Ranjit Lal is the author of over thirty-five books—fiction and non-fiction—for children and adults who are children. His abiding interest in natural history, birds, animals and insects is reflected in many of his books: *The Crow Chronicles*, *The Life and Times of Altu Faltu*, *The Small Tigers of Shergarh*, *The Birds of Delhi* and others. His book *Faces in the Water* was honoured by IBBY in 2012, won the Crossword Award for Children's Writing 2010 and the Ladli National Media Award for Gender Sensitivity 2012. *Our Nana Was a Nutcase* won the Crossword Raymond Award for Children's Writing in 2016. His other books with social themes include *Taklu and Shroom* (shortlisted for the Crossword Award for Children's Writing 2013), *Miracles*, *Smitten*, *The Secret of Falcon Heights*, *The Dugong and the Barracudas* and *The Battle for No. 19*. His other interests include photography, automobiles, reading and cooking. He lives in Delhi.

The Little NINJA Sparrows

Ranjit Lal

Illustrated by Sayantan Halder

talking
CUB

TALKING CUB

Published by Speaking Tiger Publishing Pvt. Ltd
4381/4, Ansari Road, Daryaganj
New Delhi 110002

Published in Talking Cub by Speaking Tiger in 2017
Copyright © Ranjit Lal 2017
Illustrations copyright © Sayantan Halder 2017

ISBN: 978-93-87164-46-8
eISBN: 978-93-87164-28-4

10 9 8 7 6 5 4 3 2 1

Typeset in Lora by Jojy Philip
Printed at Sanat Printers, Kundli

For Megha

Little Ninjas
in the Nest

'My dear, the last egg has finally hatched!' Shrimati Chiddya the house sparrow excitedly told her husband, Shri Churi Bahadur Chiddya. And added with pride welling over, 'And it's a little boy chick!'

Her husband looked at the revolting, naked pink wheezing blob at the bottom of the nest and stuck out his chest. 'At last! After three daughters, I have a son! I have a son!' he chirruped, strutting around. 'Blow the trumpets! Toot the horns! Bombard the social media! Let it go viral! Let everyone know! Let the celebrations begin!' He whirred down to the verandah railing and surveyed the scene before him, shouting delightedly, 'I have a son! I have a son!' till his wife had to shush him because the babies were sleeping.

Their residence, No. 1A, was located in the verandah of the fourth-floor apartment of a building called 'Sunshine Towers'. Down below was a garden studded with flowering bushes—lantana, raat-ki-raani and mehendi—bordered by trees—neem, peepal and acacia—that screened it from the road beyond. There was also a small playground and sandpit, where Churi Bahadur Chiddya and his wife (and the neighbours) sand-bathed and anted to get rid of parasites in their plumage. The residents of 'Sunshine Towers' scattered birdseed, namkeen and fruit in a feeding platform every morning.

Shri Chiddya glanced up proudly at his (disgracefully untidy) nest as his wife asked him:

'What should we call him, dear? What should we name him?'

'How about Chiddy?' he suggested. 'Chiddy Bahadur Chiddya sounds rather good!'

And so that's what the little runt was called.

The couple's three daughters—Champa, Chameli and Chamak, already hatched and squashed together in the nest—were not in the least impressed.

'Pah, now we'll have to share everything with that little squirt!' Champa said, rolling her eyes.

'And just see, Ma and Pa will bring him the fattest worms and caterpillars!' Chameli added. 'You know how goo-goo gaga they get over boys.'

'Yes, and worms and maggots with lashings of ketchup and mayo and barbeque sauce and whatnot!' Champa said disgustedly.

'Not if we can help it, girls!' Chamak smirked and promptly sat down on top of her squirming baby brother.

'Mama, Papa, we're famished!' the three hefty sisters wheezed together, opening their beaks wide. 'Feed us, feed us, feed us! We haven't eaten in fifteen minutes!'

Shri Chiddya and his good missus immediately took off to shop for baby caterpillars in the bushes below. Alone in the nest the three sisters plotted on.

'Should we just smother him and be done with it?'

'Or let him have all the hairiest spiders and prickliest caterpillars that Ma and Pa bring? He'll either choke or be allergic and no one can blame us for anything!'

'We can push him out of the nest right now and say he just fell out.'

'Nah, they'll never believe that! Besides we're supposed to be babysitting him!'

'Yeah, babysitting *on* him!' Chamak grinned, wriggling her fat bottom on top of her little brother's head.

'Bah, what a pathetic wimp!'

Sadly, Champa who had made that last remark appeared to be right. The baby boy sparrow squeaked plaintively and wriggled ineffectually at the bottom of the nest, outnumbered and outweighed by his sisters.

'Ma, tell them!' he would fuss, trying to catch his mother's attention, 'They're squishing me!' But he'd just be elbowed into a corner of the nest, or have Chamak or Champa or Chameli's fat smelly bottom in his face.

Of course, his parents did try and feed him first (with the best tidbits) when they returned from shopping trips, but invariably the three big sisters would shove and push little Chiddy to one corner, or even grab and yank out the morsel he was desperately trying to gulp down. By this time usually, their parents would have unloaded all the tender baby caterpillars, worms and spiders they had brought, and would whir off for yet another round of shopping, so they didn't really notice that their son and heir was not getting very much to eat. Also, they were hardwired to stuff the widest open mouths they could see, which needless to say belonged to Champa, Chameli and Chamak. The girls set up such a shrill, nerve-wracking ruckus (which had the same effect as a dentist's drill) that their parents just had to shut them up. And it could be dangerous if a cat or crow heard the noise and decided to investigate. Thus the runt had to be satisfied with bits and pieces of leftover worm and caterpillar and horrible splinter-like spiders' hairs that fell to the bottom of the nest. So he remained weak and small, squirming pathetically in the nest as he tried to squeeze between his overweight sisters and catch the attention of his parents.

'Why do you all hate me?' he asked his sisters one morning while their parents had taken off for another round of caterpillar shopping. 'What have I done to you?'

'We hate you because you're a boy!' Champa told him.

'And we know how parents dote over boys!'

'But that's not true! Ma and Pa don't dote over me at all! They hardly know I exist!'

'They do too! If they had their way, they'd only feed you and let us starve to death!'

'And we are not going to let that happen!'

'Girl power zindabad!'

'So sit tight and stop whining, because that's the way it's going to be!'

So little Chiddy sat tight and stopped whining. But he dreamt big dreams. One morning, he caught a glimpse of black kites diving and cavorting in the skies above and swore that when he fledged he would fly like them. He would soar in the heavens and then dive-bomb his sisters one by one, see how they liked that! He would set high-speed flying records! He'd be the best aerobatic sparrow in the world; he'd do barrel rolls and spear-dives and...and whatever other stunts falcons and swifts did! But then, one morning, he somehow managed to peep over the edge of the nest at the ground below. Far, far, far below...so far below he felt dizzy and his knees folded up and he fell back weakly to the bottom of his nest. Just what had his parents been thinking, building their home so high up in the heavens! It would take half an hour to hit the ground (with such a messy splat!), even while free-falling! He wasn't going to leave his cozy nest for anything. And yes, he decided suddenly, if he couldn't be the world's best aerobatic sparrow, he'd be the world's first (and best, needless to say) non-flying sparrow! He'd be world famous and would set an example for other sparrow-chicks who felt the same way.

Meanwhile, similar drama was being enacted in the neighbouring nest apartment (No. 2A) at the other end of the large verandah, where both these residences (1A and 2A) had been built. The only difference here was that the last to hatch in 2A was a girl sparrow.

'It's a girl,' Shrimati Bhuriya informed her husband. 'But I don't mind; we already have two sturdy boys. She can help me keep the nest clean and do Luchcha and Lafanga's laundry and homework for them!'

'Yes,' her husband agreed, 'and as soon as she fledges she can help us feed them too! Those two have the appetite of horses!'

'A girl?' Luchcha said with unpleasant glee in his voice. 'We have a baby sister?'

'Oh boy, this is going to be such fun!' his brother Lafanga added, poking his wing into his tiny sister's side. She squeaked and tried to move away only to be jostled by Luchcha on the other side.

'Hello, girlie!'

'Are we going to show you a good time, little sister!'

Their idea of a good time was this: One morning, while their parents were away, the two of them hoisted little Gouri (which is what her parents had decided to call her) up to the edge of the nest and held her over it by her tiny wings so that she dangled upside down, squeaking with terror. It was a very, very long way down. Poor little Gouri just shut her eyes and waited for the end. She was of course dumped back into the bottom of her nest by her laughing brothers, where she lay trembling and traumatized.

And needless to add, Luchcha and Lafanga monopolized all the juicy food their parents brought them, leaving only scraps for poor little

Gouri, who was also made to clean up the mess after they had eaten.

At the Chiddya residence at No. 1A, yet another distressing fact was coming to light. The one and only son and heir to the Chiddya line was showing himself to be something of a disgrace to his family's honourable name. One morning, Shri Chiddya had flown back with a really humongous wriggling McJumbo earthworm (which had been on sale)—as thick as a breakfast sausage and as long as four— and had dropped it into the nest. His wife had, at the same time, been virtually assaulted by her three daughters and had been frenziedly relieved of her load of plump caterpillars. With their beaks full, the girls couldn't deal with the giant worm immediately. It fell to the bottom of the nest with a soggy thud. Here it writhed around frantically, coiling and uncoiling, and headed in the direction of little Chiddy Bahadur Chiddya. The fledgling gave it one look and frantically backed away and squeezed himself between his two big sisters, Chamak and Chameli, trembling and squeaking with fear. He honestly thought that the earthworm was a python or anaconda and was about to devour him. Champa swallowed her caterpillar, then pounced on the worm and slurped it down gleefully like someone doing a magician's trick in reverse as Chiddy watched, nearly squashed to death between his sisters, his eyes wide with horror and beginning to feel a little sick; it was a pretty revolting sight.

'Oh...poor baby got scared by a squirmy-wormy!' Chameli sneered.

'He thought it would swallow him!' Chamak said.

'Hey Champa—the next one is ours. You hogged the whole thing, you greedy pig!'

'Yeah—but for such a noble cause, darling! It would have attacked and swallowed our baby brother, so I had to deal with it and rescue him from a horrible death!'

'We gave him protection too!' the other two laughed. 'He hid right between us, so the monster couldn't get at him! Of course, he ought to have protected the three of us from it, sacrificed his life for us even, but guys these days, I tell you!'

'I can't wait to see what's going to happen when our flying lessons begin,' Chameli said gleefully. 'The dude is going to have a complete meltdown!'

'Papa said he's hired a personal trainer for us who will make us exercise and teach us yoga and give us flying lessons,' Chamak added. Indeed it was so. In the 'old' days, most baby birds exercised their wings on their own and learnt to fly with the enthusiastic encouragement (and a lot of shouting) from their doting parents. Not any longer. Nowadays all elite bird families employed personal trainers for the task. These trainers would teach the chicks wing exercises, the theory of aerodynamics and flight, rules of the sky, navigation by night and day using the stars and sun and finally flight itself.

'Little bro, you know, very soon you'll have to hop to the edge of the nest and jump off, and we're on the fourth floor!' Champak maliciously told little Chiddy who was listening to the conversation with rising horror. She went on, 'How about that? It's a very long way down and there's sure to be tomcats waiting below, whipping their tails back and forth and yowling! They always hang around when there are flying lessons being given.'

'What?' Chiddy squeaked, 'But I get vertigo if I stand up inside the nest!'

'Wonder what this trainer guy is like...' Chameli mused. 'Will he be handsome? Will he be rich?'

'Hope he is!' Chamak said.

He was.

As soon as the youngsters had fledged, Shri Chiddya brought the trainer over to meet his brood.

'Girls, I want you to meet Flt Lt (Retd) Tezhawa Pankha who will teach you how to fly like no sparrow has flown before,' Shri Chiddya said as he introduced the trainer to his family. He went on, 'He has just retired from the NSAF (National Sparrow Air-Force) after a very distinguished flying career. He has flown over 12,500 sorties between flashing ceiling-fan blades without incident. He has diced with death on a daily basis but has not been diced yet! Sir, these are my daughters—and that little fellow, my son! All yours! Turn them into maestros of the sky!'

'It will be my pleasure, sir!' Flt Lt Pankha chirruped, eyeing the three hefty girls with approval. 'So when do you want me to start? I'm coming this side to teach the two boys and one little girl in No. 2A next door every morning at seven...so can start with your kids at eight. Will that be suitable?'

It was and soon all was fixed. The three girls in No. 1A had stars in their eyes.

'Oh my God, I'd fly to the moon for him!'

'I'd fly to Mars and Venus!'

'Jupiter, Neptune, Pluto!'

'Thank you, Papa, thank you.'

'We love you!'

Little Chiddy however, had eyed the burly Flt Lt (Retd) Tez-hawa Pankha with great trepidation. The muscle-bound trainer had rested his beady eyes on him briefly, but it was enough. The little sparrow knew he was in for a tough time. He thought of how far below the ground was and felt nauseous. A determined glint entered the little sparrow's eyes. He knew what he was going (or rather not going) to do.

'But Mama, do I *have* to learn how to fly?' little Gouri plaintively asked her mother in No. 2A next door. 'I'm quite happy here and don't want to go anywhere.' She swallowed, trying not to remember the terror when her brothers had dangled her over the edge of the nest.

'Don't be so silly! Of course you have to learn!' her mother replied impatiently. 'Look at your brothers—they can hardly wait to take off. And that strong, handsome Flt Lt Tez will teach you everything you need to know about flying. Huh! You have no idea how lucky you are—when I was a little girl, I had to learn everything on my own...'

'But I don't want to learn! And I don't think he's handsome either! He looks like a bully! He's got mean, piggy eyes!'

'Hush! Don't say such things.'

Gouri's brothers, Luchcha and Lafanga, were of course thrilled with the prospect.

'You know,' Luchcha said, 'Papa said he's also teaching the chicks next door how to fly! We'd better learn before they do!'

were being eagerly looked forward to by a new generation of sparrows. Not all of them, of course, but well, nearly all of them.

The No-fly Revolution

The flying lessons started punctually at 7 the next morning at No. 2A. Luchcha and Lafanga were beside themselves with excitement, while little Gouri just shut her eyes tightly and pretended to be asleep. Flt Lt (Retd) Tez-hawa Pankha eyed his pupils keenly. The parent birds had taken off for their regular morning flight and for (a free) breakfast at a nearby bird feeder.

'Right boys, look lively. Up on the nest's edge, NOW! Ten-hun!'

'Yessir, yessir, right away sir,' the boys gabbled, hoisting themselves up to the edge of the nest. They saluted their trainer with their wings.

'Miss, I'm waiting! I don't have all day!'

'Sir...I have a headache in my tummy!' Gouri squeaked.

'Get out of there and come up on the edge, NOW!'

'Yeah, get a move on, Gouri!' Lafanga shouted.

'We want to start!' Luchcha added.

Trembling, Gouri hoisted herself up to the nest's edge, not daring to look down.

Flt Lt Tez eyed them up and down.

'Look at you!' he bellowed. 'Fat, obese, overweight, all you do is lie in the nest and stuff your faces! Now, give me 500 flap-and-hops!'

'What...sir? Flap and hops?'

'Yes, like this! Watch me!'

Flt Lt Tez extended his wings, flapped them and hopped lightly at the same time. 'Come on, 1...2...3... move it, move it, move it, jump, jump, jump!'

Luchcha and Lafanga hopped clumsily and tried flapping.

'Heck, I can do one or the other!' Luchcha panted. 'Either hop or flap!'

'Or flap but not hop!'

'Not hop and flap together!' Luchcha reiterated.

Poor little Gouri tried and pitched backwards into the nest. Here she remained, scrunched up in a little feathery ball, hoping the trainer would not notice her and just go away. No such luck.

'Miss, get out of there!' he roared, looming over the edge of the nest and yanking her out by her pinions. 'Now get to work!'

Needless to say by the end of the hour all three sparrow chicks were completely exhausted and flopped down at the bottom of their nest, wheezing and panting.

'You're all in terrible shape!' Flt Lt Tez sneered. 'You will all repeat these exercises after every hour.

You need to build stamina and strength. At the moment you can't even lift your fat butts an inch off the ground! You should be ashamed!'

He then flew off to No. 1A to tackle Champa, Chameli, Chamak and little Chiddy.

'Right girls, let's see what you can do! On to the edge of the nest on the double! Face outwards! You too mister! Let's see if you ladies can do better than those fat lazy bums next door!'

'Yes, sir!'

'Sure, sir!'

'Can do, sir!'

'Will do, sir!'

'Isn't he cute?' Chamak whispered to her sisters who giggled.

Chiddy perched at the edge of the nest and shut his eyes, trying desperately to keep his balance. His three hefty sisters had started jumping up and down vigorously, and were upsetting the stability of the nest.

'Eyes front!' barked Flt Lt Tez. Chiddy opened his eyes and made the mistake of glancing down. He pitched forward. Flt Lt Tez's hefty wing slammed against his chest and shoved him back into the nest.

'Did I tell you to jump?' he yelled. 'You don't jump out of the nest until I tell you to jump. Savvy?'

'Dd...ddizzy...vertigo...' stammered Chiddy.

'Nonsense! No bird suffers from vertigo!'

'Bb...bbut...'

'You want to be one of those shameless things—a flightless bird?'

'N...no sir!' (But of course, he did!)

'Then flap your wings and jump up and down!' the Flt Lt yelled. 'Look at your sisters! They're giving it their all! Way to go girls, way to go!'

But for little Chiddy Bahadur Chiddya it was not the way to go.

As the lessons went on, the chicks' parents would often perch on the verandah railings and watch them fondly.

'He'll have them up and flying in no time at all!' Shri Chiddya said approvingly.

'Hmm...all except Chiddy, I fear,' his wife said. 'Maybe he should just stay behind in the nest...'

'Don't be silly. We have to raise another brood soon!'

'Just as well we found this guy!' Shri Chiddya said to the parents of Luchcha, Lafanga and Gouri. 'He'll teach them all the tricks of the trade: how to fly through flashing ceiling-fan blades and windmills, or evade hawks and crows and cats and pebbles from catapults.'

'How are your girls coping?' Gouri's mother asked Shrimati Chiddya.

'The girls are doing great, it's the little boy we're worried about,' Shrimati Chiddya admitted. 'He's umm...doesn't seem to be made out for this sort of thing.'

'Like my little Gouri—but at least she's a girl.'

'Boy or girl, they have to learn how to fly!'

The lessons continued daily, with homework (both practical and theory) also given every day. Physical training, wing exercises, and stamina-building was accompanied by lectures on the theory of flight, the science of aerodynamics, navigation by day and night (though sparrows didn't really use this too much), wing-and-feather design and biology, evasive tactics and the history of bird flight, yoga and meditation.

'What is it that makes us birds?' Flt Lt Tez roared during one of the theory lectures. 'It is the fact that we can fly! Of course there are some birds that can't or don't fly—but they are a disgrace to the bird kingdom! It is flight that gives us freedom—we can come and go where and when we want. Some of us fly 25,000 km every year over oceans and continents! You all know about our magnificent migratory flights every year! When human beings "fly", they need passports, visas and tickets and have to spend three hours getting to the airport and waiting three hours there and go through humiliating security checks and strip searches, and then are locked up in long aluminium tubes for however long their flight takes. And then it takes them three more hours to clear customs and immigration—a really primitive way of travel, if you ask me! We just spread our wings and go! That is why human beings and other creatures are so envious of us. They can't fly freely! We can! Remember that!'

Needless to add, Chiddy and Gouri excelled in theory and their homework exercises were shamelessly copied by their elder siblings. In the practicals, alas, they didn't fare nearly as well. And then all too soon, it was time to take-off, time for the first test flight: who would pass? Who would fail and be made to repeat the lessons? Who would be given the precious flying licence and certificate of airworthiness, and who would have to repeat the exam? The day of the first flight dawned bright and sunny with good visibility but with a mischievous huff-and-puff breeze (whose name was Breaking Wind) blowing.

'Right girls, let's see what you can do!' Flt Lt Tez barked. From the neighbouring nest, Luchcha and Lafanga watched, jeering and leering. Actually they were a little nervous because it would be their turn next.

Flt Lt Tez flew down to a huge bougainvillea bush in the garden below and perched on top of it.

'Right, you, Ms Champa—you're first. Fly down to me!'

'Yes, sir.' She shut her eyes, fluttered her wings and jumped with a little scream. She crash landed in a mehendi bush, far too short, the breath whooshing out of her. From its midst she struggled to hop to its top. A garden lizard, sunning itself on the top of the bush, eyed her sardonically and scuttled away.

'Not enough airspeed, you stalled!' Flt Lt Tez yelled at her. 'You'll have to try again. Get right to the top of that bush and try again! Now you, Ms Chameli.'

Poor Chameli took off and was huffed and puffed at by Breaking Wind (chuckling away) erratically towards an adjoining balcony railing on the third floor, to which she clung for dear life, her plumage a complete mess.

'Crosswinds! Wind shear! You got hit by a crosswind and wind shear and they blew you off course! Always be prepared for that. Now you, Ms Chamak!'

Chamak took a deep breath, shut her eyes, jumped and flapped her wings furiously. Then she opened her eyes, corrected her course and headed straight for her coach.

'Catch me, sir, catch me!' she screamed as she fluttered down, her wings blurring. She collided right into him with a soft 'whump'. He staggered back but held her firmly.

'Oh sir, you saved me, you saved me!'

'Humph, very well...you had speed and direction only you have to learn how to land properly. You can't collide into others and knock them over every time you land.'

'I don't mind colliding into you every time I land, sir,' Chamak murmured as her sisters giggled.

'Hey now, where's the runt?' the Flt Lt asked, disengaging himself from Chamak. 'It's his turn!'

But the runt Chiddy had decided that come what may, he would not fly today or ever. He would be the world's first flightless sparrow! He just stayed put in his nest even as Flt Lt Tez bawled him out, his father angrily informed him that he was a disgrace to the family and would be disinherited and his mother wept buckets of tears and tried heavy emotional blackmail.

'I don't want to learn how to fly!' he said stubbornly, crouching low in the nest, remembering how his tummy had churned when he had looked down. 'Not now, not ever! You can't make me! I'm on satyagraha like Gandhiji, so there! I'm going to be the world's first and only flightless sparrow!'

'One day!' his father raved, 'One day, I will just throw you out of the nest! See how you like that! You are a disgrace to the Chiddya clan!'

'Let him be, dear,' his mother sniffed and then turned to her stubborn son, her eyes glimmering with tears. 'Though really, beta, what will everyone say? And just think: who will want to marry your sisters? They'll be left bitter, lonely spinsters all their lives with no babies to look after! Be brave, darling, and do it just for me!'

'No Ma, I don't want to and I'm not going to!'

'Let him be!' Flt Lt Tez said disgusted. 'He'll fly

when he wants to, if ever! Now I have another test to take, so excuse me!'

He flew across the verandah to his other pupils in No. 2A. Chamak, Chameli and Champa watched as Luchcha and Lafanga got ready for their test flight, flexing their pinions and trying to look as cool as the fighter pilots in *Top Gun*. Little Gouri cowered at the bottom of the nest, determined (like Chiddy) not to fly.

'Okay, boys go—you, Lafanga, first!' barked Flt Lt Tez as Chamak hopped up close to him again.

Lafanga leapt high, fluttered his wings powerfully, kept one eye on Champa still perched on the mehendi bush and headed straight for her. He crashed well short of the bush onto the grass, bounced up and began strutting around with his chest stuck out.

Luchcha, not to be outdone, took off and flew erratically right into poor Chameli, perched on her third-floor verandah railing, knocking her head over heels right into the verandah. Luckily the flat was empty.

'Look where you're going, you idiot!' she remonstrated but not angrily. With the help of a potted plant nearby both of them hopped back onto the railing.

'Where's the little girlie?' Flt Lt Tez now asked looking around.

'She doesn't want to fly!'

'She's hiding in the nest!'

'What? Another anti-flight protester? Good god! What is this new generation coming to? All they want to do is stay at home and play video games or surf the net! Very well, at least you five have passed and will get your flying licences and airworthiness certificates tomorrow. The other two, I am afraid, have failed and will have to try again! Good day!' And with that Flt Lt Tez took off, with Chamak trailing erratically and valiantly behind him, calling out, 'Wait for me, sir! Wait for me!'

At No. 1A, Shri Chiddya was still extremely upset. While he was proud of his daughters, he was hugely ashamed of his son. He felt humiliated.

'He's taken after your side of the family,' he

angrily told his wife, 'we don't have such cowards in our family!'

'My family?' his wife shrilled, bristling. 'Don't you dare accuse my family members of being cowards! My father had more guts than your entire clan ever had! He won the Sunheri Bajra Medal of Honour for Valour after pecking a tomcat on the ear while on a daring sortie during the great Billi Wars! Your father did nothing of the kind.'

At No. 2A, Shrimati Bhuriya looked worriedly at her little daughter, crouched at the bottom of the nest, stubborn silver tears gleaming like pearls in her dark eyes. Of course the little girl helped out with the nest-work, but eventually she would have to get married and leave the nest. If she could not fly, that would be impossible.

'What should we do with her?' she asked her husband worriedly. 'She's quite happy sitting there at the bottom of the nest eating the boys' leftovers and tidying up. Who will marry her?'

'Well, at least the boys have done well,' Shri Bhuriya said. And added, 'Not like the fellow in

1A—Shri Chiddya has a wimp of a son. Just imagine! Chiddya can't show his face anywhere.' He went on proudly, 'And already our boys are chasing those girls next door!'

'Hmm...' his wife said disapprovingly, 'those three sisters are a bit too fast and loose for my liking. Not homely!'

At the bottom of the nest at No. 1A Chiddy Bahadur Chiddya crouched down and shut his ears and eyes to the taunts of his three sisters and the hectoring of his father.

'Chiddy, hear this, because I shall say this only once!' his father shouted towering over him, and waving his wings in his face and sticking his chest out belligerently. 'Flt Lt Tez has kindly agreed to conduct your test again—tomorrow morning. You will stand on the rim of the nest and you will jump off it. You will fly even if it is the last thing that you do. I will accept nothing else. If you refuse, I will kick you off myself and disown you thereafter. Is that clear? No son of mine is a coward! You have humiliated me!'

'Cowardly custard!' his sisters taunted him gleefully. 'Little baba is scared of heights!'

Chiddy Bahadur Chiddya said nothing. But he was thinking: there was only one thing to do—leave home. He would have to leave the nest, get down to the ground somehow, and hop away into hiding. And never come back.

Slowly, a plan formed in his head. Early next morning—even before the magpie robin next door began his sweet morning melody—he would go to the rim of the nest and somehow climb down the bougainvillea creeper, before anyone in the family awoke. And disappear forever.

'Beti, you will just have to learn how to fly,' Shrimati Bhuriya was telling her little daughter. 'Who will marry you otherwise? Your bhaiyyas will help you if you like!'

'Yeah, like we'll dangle you right over and then drop you, so you'll have to fly or fall on your head!' Luchcha said, nudging his brother.

'Yeah, a heave-ho and down she'll go! Topsy-turvy, rumble-tumble, humpty-dumpty, we all fall down!'

And poor little Gouri's heart pounded horribly inside her. She knew her brothers were quite capable of doing what they said. She had to get away from here. From those horrible, mean louts.

too much. Why couldn't they just leave her alone?

Slowly a plan formed in her little head. Early next morning, before that sweet bird nearby began whistling, she would awake, go to the rim of her nest and just jump down and hope for the best. She

Dear Mama,

I've gone. Now you don't have to worry about me (sob!) ever again! I'm never coming back (sob!). Goodbye! Love and kisses to everyone! Your loving daughter, G!

And that would be that.

Running Away

There was commotion in the two sparrows' homes early next morning.

'Hey, where's the runt?' Chamak asked looking around as she awoke. 'Chameli, are you sitting on him?'

'No! Maybe Champa had him for a midnight snack!' Chameli giggled.

'No way—he'd be way too bony.' They looked around the nest. Where the heck was he?

Their parents, who had been roosting just nearby in the bougainvillea creeper that swarmed up the side of the verandah, were stretching their wings and preparing for their daily morning flight and breakfast round when the girls told them the news.

'Ma, Pa—the runt's disappeared!' the girls shrieked. 'Chiddy's gone!'

'He's run away from his flying test today!'

Shri Chiddya was furious. 'He's done the bunk, playing hooky! He'll be back after Flt Lt Tez leaves! Then I'll have his hide!'

'I hope you're right dear and he does return!' Chiddy's mother said, worriedly. 'Though I wonder if he'll be able to survive on his own even for a little while! He can't even fly! The cats or owls or crows are sure to get him. Maybe we and the girls ought to look for him.'

The three girls looked at each other, wondering why they seemed to have got a sudden lump in their throats and why they were feeling strangely uncomfortable. They gulped.

'You know,' Champa said *sotto voce*, 'I don't know about you two but I'm kind of missing the pipsqueak already! The nest seems sort of empty without him...no one to sit on, if you know what I mean.'

'Yeah, me too.'

'Do you think we teased him too much?'

'He was so easy to tease!'

'We were pretty horrible to him!'

'And so mean!'

'He was such a scaredy booby!'

'And such a baby!'

'Well, he did defy Papa and Flt Lt Tez and refused to fly. He stuck to his guns. That shows character and guts.'

'Wonder where he is now?'

'Poor little fellow.'

'He must be scared and hungry.'

'Ma...should we go and look for Chiddy?' Chamak asked, quickly wiping a glistening tear.

'Bah!' her father retorted. 'Bah! You girls will do no such thing. He'll come back with his tail between his legs when he's ready!'

At 2A next door, Shrimati Bhuriya too was quite upset. She had awoken and was shocked to find little Gouri missing from the nest. Suddenly she realized just how fond she had been of her timid little daughter—and was beginning to miss her a great deal. She read and re-read little Gouri's note again and again.

'You boys ought not to have teased her so much,' she said tearfully, turning over the note, 'you made her run away! And she's such a tiny little thing—the rats and even cockroaches will get her in no time at all.'

'Would you like us to search for her?' Lafanga asked doubtfully. Truth be told, both the brothers had suddenly found that they too were missing their little sister and were feeling a bit bad. Sure they had teased and ragged her unmercifully and had done that horrible thing to her, but they didn't want something nasty to happen to her either—

like becoming breakfast for some giant cockroach or ghastly bandicoot. Who would they tease then? Besides, *they* had the right to tease her all they wanted—they were family after all—but no one else had the right to touch a feather on her head. The family would see to that.

'We'll all search for her,' their mother said. 'She couldn't fly so couldn't have gone very far. I just hope we find her before it's too late!' Search, they did, but there was no trace of the little sparrow anywhere. She had vanished!

And where indeed were the two little runaway sparrows and what had become of them?

Chiddy had left the nest as early as 4 a.m. It had been pitch dark, but he had sensed the coming dawn—not that he had slept much that night at all. He had been too full of dark emotion for that. He hated his father for getting on his case in the way he had. As for his three sisters, all they had ever done for him was to rag him wretched. Well, he'd show them! He'd run away and never come back. See how they liked that! He squirmed his way past his plump sleeping sisters to the edge of the nest, feeling his way along with his wings and claws. Cautiously the little sparrow hopped his way down the many intertwined branches of the immense bougainvillea creeper—occasionally wincing as he confronted the fearsome thorns with which the plant had armed itself. Once or twice, he slipped and free-fell down for a bit before a branch caught him and jerked him to a stop. He was still some way up from the ground when he felt himself falling again. He glanced down: in the hazy orange-gold light of a sodium vapour mast light nearby, he saw an array of sharply curved thorns, like spear blades, directly below him. He'd be impaled, indeed skewered if he landed on them!

'Oh, God!' he squawked, shutting his eyes and waiting for the inevitable. And then a sudden, gust of wind (our old friend Breaking Wind no less!) who had been loafing about looking for victims for his pranks, caught him unawares and whisked him off as though he had been a dandelion or a parasailing spiderling.

'Oopsadaisy, and up we go!' Breaking Wind said kindly, 'You're too young to become a seekh kebab, my friend!'

Chiddy squawked in surprise and flapped his tiny wings furiously, but the powerful gust just blew him up, up and away, over the garden and wall, across the road and beyond. It swept the little sparrow up and down, as if he were on an airborne roller coaster for quite some time, over roads and gardens and houses. Suddenly, Breaking Wind just lost interest (as was his wont) and dropped dead in his tracks and gently deposited the frantically flapping, gasping little sparrow on the ground several kilometers away from the creeper on 'Sunshine Towers' where his home had been.

'See ya later, kid,' he said, 'there's a cool breezy little thing coming this way and I want to meet her! You'll be safe here!'

Chiddy landed softly and rolled over and over like a little fluffball before crouching low, trying to catch his breath and wondering where he was and what to do next. He had absolutely no idea.

Little Gouri too had awoken at about the same time as Chiddy had. Her nest had been constructed at the other end of the fourth-floor verandah in the small gap between a pair of fat water pipes that went all the way down to the ground floor. There was a tiny gap between the parallel pipes and the wall to which they were affixed and it was into this gap that the little sparrow squeezed herself and began sliding down slowly, like a climber doing a 'chimney' climb in reverse. The rough wall and pipe scraped against her delicate soft plumage, but she remained determined. But then, when she had reached about the second floor, the gap between the pipes and the wall suddenly and inexplicably widened and little Gouri found that she was free-falling, just as Chiddy had. She fluttered her little wings frantically in panic, and at exactly this moment, Breaking Wind who had picked up Chiddy, caught her too, lifted her up effortlessly and carried her high, high, high up into the pre-dawn sky. Then he dropped little Gouri, taken by surprise again, plummeted down like a badminton shuttlecock and she landed on her little bottom with an almighty thump that drove the breath out of her. Peeping plaintively, she looked around but it was still dark—and she couldn't make anything out. Like Chiddy, she had no idea where she was or what she was going to do next.

Actually it wasn't too long before the two little runaway sparrows realized what they had to do next:

Eat!

They were hungry! Famished and ravenous!

And the prospect of finding food, let alone being fed, seemed bleak. At least in their own nests they had managed on leftovers and sometimes got almost whole caterpillars or crispy spiders' legs. But their moms had warned them that this spoon-feeding would end when they left the nest. They'd have to fend for themselves and god forbid, largely become something called vegetarian—eating grain and seeds. And now it seemed as if that time had come!

Dawn had broken, the sky turning pink, gold and orange and along with it, the morning chorus of birds had begun. Bulbuls whistled cheerily, magpie-robins gave soulful flute concertos, tailor-birds shouted as excitedly as hawkers, sunbirds performed like rockstars—and of course parakeets, babblers and mynas simply added to the general morning bustle and hubbub, as they exchanged greetings. Song and music was all very well and may have been spiritually uplifting—but did little to assuage the pangs of hunger that gnawed at the little birds' tummies. Cautiously then, both the runaway sparrows got to their feet and began checking out their surroundings, as the light improved. Which is when they got the happiest surprise of that morning so far. Scattered on the ground everywhere were delicious looking golden-yellow pearl-like seeds. They got so busy picking these up and scoffing them that they suddenly backed into one another with a soft bump.

'Uh!' grunted Chiddy, straightening up and looking over his shoulder.

'Eek—look where you're going, you moron!' Gouri protested.

The two sparrows stared at each other in surprise.

'And you are?' Gouri asked raising her eyebrows.

'Myself Chiddy Bahadur Chiddya at your service—and your good name is?'

'Gouri! What are you doing here?'

'Having breakfast! And you?'

'What does it look like, dodo?'

'Where's your family? What's a little girl like you doing out and about all by herself so early in the morning? Don't you know there may be cats and bandicoots around?'

'What I'm doing here is for me to know and you to find out. And I may ask the same question of you!'

Chiddy sighed. 'I left home,' he muttered. 'They... they didn't want me!'

'You're a flyaway?'

'Technically, no—but spiritually, yes!'

'I left home too! I'm a runaway too!'

They stared at each other.

'You...you just flew out of your nest?' Gouri asked.

'Uh...technically, no! They wanted me to fly—tried to force me.' He straightened himself up to his maximum height. 'And no once forces Chiddy Bahadur Chiddya to do anything against his will. I'm my own bird. So I just climbed down—and then this gust of wind picked me up and deposited me here.'

'You booked a gust of wind to pick you up and drop you here like it was a radio cab?' Gouri was impressed.

'Uh...no, not exactly...it just turned up! Lucky for me or I would have fallen on a bunch of thorns.'

'I can't fly either,' Gouri admitted sweetly and understanding completely. 'I'm terrified of flying. My brothers were threatening to dangle me upside down over the side of the nest and drop me into the jaws of cats waiting below. So I left. That wind caught me too.'

'Where did you live?'

'"Sunshine Towers", fourth floor No. 2A.'

'Oh, I'm in 1A—we were neighbours, just imagine!'

'And now here we are!'

'Which is exactly where?'

'Dunno! But there's plenty of birdseed lying around! Help yourself!'

Gouri eyed him sardonically. 'You go first— you're pretty scrawny looking. Your need is greater than mine!'

'You're pretty anorexic too if I may say so,' Chiddy responded. 'All your bones are sticking out! Are you on one of those crazy diet things? Or do you regurgitate everything you eat?'

'Oh stop talking so much and start eating!'

'Wak-wak-wak-wak-wak! So what do we have here?' suddenly clucked a loud, but not unkind voice from very close by. 'Wak-wak-wak—what on earth are you two doing in our chicken run apart from scoffing our breakfast?'

Clinging together the two little sparrows looked up. An enormous brown bird with silky maroon-umber feathers, and scaly yellow legs was appraising them out of enquiring eyes, cocking its head this way and that.

'Gg...ggood morning, ma'am...we...we were

blown in here by the wind...' Gouri stuttered as Chiddy nodded. 'S...so sorry about that!'

'Wh...where are we, ma'am?' Chiddy dared ask.

'In a chicken run dear, right next to a chicken coop, where else? Thankfully not in a chicken soup! Though really it's high time someone wrote a book called, *Chicken Soup for the Chicken's Soul*, don't you think? Ah, but I'm digressing now... And you sweet things are?'

'My name is Gouri, ma'am!'

'Chiddy Bahadur Chiddya, ma'am!'

'Ah, and you can call me Murgiben auntieji. You two have run away together?' Murgiben clucked disapprovingly. 'At such a young age! Really. What is this generation coming to?'

'No, ma'am, er...well yes, sort of!' Chiddy stammered.

'We ran away, but not together,' Gouri clarified.

'We only just met!'

'And may I enquire why you ran away?' Murgiben asked delicately, 'If that is not too personal a question?'

'Fear of flying' Gouri admitted. 'We're scared of flying.'

'She's scared—not me!' Chiddy said, 'I just wasn't in the mood to fly and they tried to force me. So I showed them!'

'By running away? Ah, yes I see. The impetuousness of youth! Flying? That's kind of overrated my dears, don't you think? Look at us chickens—we run around everywhere and only fly as a last resort. It's so fatiguing dear, simply not worth the effort.'

The two little runaways looked around. They were in a fenced in chicken run, with a green wooden chicken coop at one end. A stream of golden fluff-balls emerged from the coop and ran up to Murgiben auntieji cheeping excitedly.

'Ah, meet the brood!' Murgiben said, as the chicks gathered around her and began pecking at the seed lying on the ground. Then they surrounded Gouri and Chiddy, eyeing them curiously.

'They're refugees, dears,' Murgiben informed her chicks. 'They're seeking asylum here. We have to give them sanctuary! Say hello to them now, babies.'

A chorus of friendly, if slightly shy, 'hellos' broke out.

'Mama—are they here for the Treatment too? Will they be given the Treatment too?' one of the chicks asked. 'They said today—so they should begin it anytime soon now! We're so excited!'

'As they are here I suppose they will be given the Treatment!' Murgiben said softly, nodding her head. 'Every chick here gets the Treatment, you know that... But really it's such a beautiful Treatment so they won't mind at all! How can anyone object to it? They're lucky!'

'Yes, and so are we!'

'Lucky, lucky, lucky!'

Gouri and Chiddy eyed each other.

'Er...ma'am...exactly what is this Treatment?' Gouri asked, somehow not quite liking the sound of this unknown 'lucky' Treatment with a capital T.

'You'll find out, dear! We'll keep it as a surprise for you! How about that? Now help yourself to

It's very nutritious.'

Industriously the chicks began helping themselves to the golden chickenfeed cornmeal scattered on the ground, while Murgiben clucked fussily around them, her bronze plumage glistening in the sun.

The Treatment and Capture

The surprise unfolded with terrifying rapidity some time later that morning. There came a loud rattling sound, and then a pair of gigantic feet clad in scruffy trainers stomped up to them in the chicken run. A voice shouted 'shoo-shoo-shoo!' and herded Murgiben and the fluff-balls and the two refugee sparrows into the chicken coop. Soon afterwards

a couple of hairy hands thrust themselves inside the coop and expertly scooped up, two at a time, all the golden fluff-balls—as well as poor Gouri and Chiddy.

'Yeh dekh!' a harsh voice exclaimed, 'Inko bhi kar do—we'll do them too!' So along with the chicks the sparrows were dumped into a large cloth bag, which became all dim and dark as the string was drawn. They heard the coop door clang shut and in the distance, Murgiben auntieji cluck them farewell:

'Goodbye dears! Have a good time!'

'Urrghmf...' Chiddy grunted trying to get some fluffy down feathers out of his face, in the darkness. 'Gouri—are you okay?'

'Mmmf...yes...Chiddy what's going to happen to us?'

'We're going for the Treatment at last!' one of the chicks squeaked happily sitting virtually on poor Gouri's head. 'They're taking us for the Treatment!'

'I thought it would never happen!'

'The Treatment, the Treatment, three cheers for the Treatment!'

A little while later, the drawstring of the bag was opened and a hairy hand thrust itself inside again. It grabbed a handful of chicks—maybe four— and withdrew. After a few moments the procedure was repeated.

'Stay next to me, please, Chiddy,' Gouri pleaded. 'We're in this together...'

'I don't like the feel of this,' Chiddy muttered. 'Not one bit...'

He certainly didn't like the feel of it when a rough hand grasped him and little Gouri and withdrew, clutching them both. And then they were out of the bag, blinking in the bright lights and looking around. They were in a decrepit-looking room with peeling grey walls, which was lined with bird cages. All the cages were stuffed with multicoloured birds cheeping, tweeting and hopping around. On a long wooden table nearby were a series of large tin cans. Each had a coloured liquid gleaming in it: bright turquoise blue, magenta, pillar-box red, sunflower yellow, mauve, indigo, forest green, shocking pink, purple and even silver and gold!

'Kya rang?' The question was asked by the person holding on to Gouri and Chiddy.

'Lal!' said another voice.

And suddenly the little sparrow chicks found themselves beak-deep in a foul-smelling ruby red liquid. They desperately kept their beaks shut so they wouldn't swallow any of the glutinous stuff.

'Help, I can't swim!' Gouri spluttered, flapping her tiny wings frantically.

'Do they think we're ducklings?' Chiddy gulped, spouting out a mouthful of ghastly liquid.

'We're going to drown!' Gouri gasped, going under.

But they didn't drown. A net scooped them out of the liquid and plonked them on another table spread with old newspaper. Wet and bedraggled, the little sparrows just sat there woebegone, trying to comprehend what had just happened. They eyed each other incredulously.

'Oh my God, Yo...you're bright red—from...from head to toe!' Gouri stuttered. 'You look weird! Like nothing on earth!'

'You too!' Chiddy said. 'You look like you've had a bloodbath!'

'No...no one will recognize us like this!'

'Oh God, what do we do now?'

They looked around again. The little golden fluff-balls that had also been dipped in the colours didn't appear to be upset at all. Indeed they seemed to be thrilled. They pranced and preened around and pirouetted on the newspaper as they dried themselves off.

'Ooo...look at me! Mauve! It's my favourite colour!'

'And I'm magenta! Mmmma...genta!' gushed another. 'I look like a fuchsia!'

'And I'm a golden girl! Beat that if you can!'

They strutted around happily as the sun dried the dye on them.

And all too soon, poor Gouri and Chiddy were caught once again and thrust into a tiny cage.

'Inn dono ko doosre se alag—put these two separately from the others,' a voice ordered as Gouri and Chiddy were pushed into the cage, and the door slammed shut. 'Take them to India Gate. I want not less than Rs 200 each for them, understand?'

A rough-looking man with a coarse stubble and crooked yellow teeth grabbed their cage, and along with several others piled them on his bicycle's carrier and set off on a terrifying journey through the congested, noisy streets of Old Delhi, heading towards India Gate.

'This is terrible!' Gouri said softly, burying her face in Chiddy's shoulder.

'We're birds—and we've been caged!'

'We can't fly anywhere,' Chiddy said and then looked at his new friend with stricken eyes.

'We didn't want to fly—now we'll never have to!' Gouri said softly. 'And never be able to!'

'To fly—that's what makes us birds!' Chiddy said righteously, feeling a prick of guilt that he tried to ignore, 'No matter what Murgiben auntieji said about flight being overrated!' Or that he had thought about being the world's first flightless sparrow.

'We're birds, and we ought to be free,' Gouri agreed. 'Remember what Flt Lt Tez told us?'

'Umm...I have a confession to make,' Chiddy said in a low voice. 'You know I never actually learned how to fly. I never flew. Not once! I wanted to be the world's first flightless sparrow. But now I wish I had tried. Now I can't fly and I don't know how to!'

'Me neither! I was too scared. But now I want to fly more than anything else,' Gouri admitted.

But it didn't seem as though their wishes were going to come true anytime soon.

India Gate was cacophonous and terrifying and swarming with people: sightseers, evening walkers, and hawkers selling everything from giant multi-coloured balloons to golgappas and candyfloss, urchins scampering around and diving into the ponds, tourists from near and afar, families having picnics. Everyone seemed to be shouting and shoving. The fellow who had taken their cage parked his bicycle near the great monument. He held up the cage so passers-by could see Chiddy and Gouri. Several people stopped and peered at them, some even asked how much they cost, but no one bought them.

At last a kind (if glum) faced gentleman with a thin moustache and curly hair stopped beside them. He was glum because he had forgotten it had been his little daughter, Ashiana's, tenth birthday that day, and had just been given a rocket by his wife who had called him up and yelled, 'You'd better not come home without a present for her! She's very upset!' Now he peered at the two little 'red' sparrows, enchanted.

'What are they?' he asked the hawker.

'Splendid Rubybirds, sirji,' the man responded without batting an eyelid, 'Very rare birds!'

'How much?'

'Only Rs 350 each...'

They settled for Rs 225 each and pleased with his purchase, Ashiana's father set off home with a gift for his daughter. He knew she would be thrilled. He was right.

'They're beautiful, Papa!' she cried, clapping her hands with delight and hugging him, when he presented them to her. 'Thank you!' She was a sweet-faced, toothy little girl with large soulful eyes and soft brown hair that fell to her shoulders. Enchanted, she gazed at Chiddy and Gouri. 'What are they, Papa?' she asked.

'They're called Splendid Rubybirds,' her father said, 'They're very rare birds!'

'They really do look like rubies, don't they?' Ashiana exclaimed, her eyes glowing. 'What do they eat?'

'The fellow said wheat, bajra and birdseed! I've bought a packet!'

'I'll hang their cage up in the balcony,' the little girl said and proceeded to do so, 'Then they'll be able to see the other birds and won't be lonely!'

And so, little Gouri and Chiddy found themselves in a cage hanging in the balcony of a building, at the other end of the city from 'Sunshine Towers' where their own nests had been. A newspaper was spread on the floor of the cage. Every morning the maid, a rather grim, hatchet-faced lady, thrust her hand into the cage to fill up the food bowl or change the water and newspaper, while Ashiana stood by and helped her. Then the sparrows were left very much to themselves the entire day. At first, before leaving for school, and often after she got back home, Ashiana would gaze at them happily, and even talk to them and tell them about her day at school—but well they were not parrots and so couldn't talk back to her. Eventually, she got a little bored with them and stopped spending so much time with them, letting her maid do all the feeding and cleaning.

It wasn't too bad really—because at least Happy, the family's big benign black Labrador, would settle down beneath their cage and keep them company through the day. (He was lonely too, because there was no one at home most of the day.) When they chirruped to each other he would cock his ears and tilt his head from side to side and softly whine in agreement, his brown eyes raised upwards towards them.

What was terrible however was how other birds—sparrows, munias, parakeets, babblers and mynas et al would occasionally turn up in the balcony and jeer and mock at them. Crows would even try to thrust their horrible, and very dangerous, beaks into the cage to peck at them.

'Look what we've got here!' the other birds jeered. 'A pair of jailbirds! What are you in for, darlings? Crapping on a Mercedes' windshield?'

And then alas, one of the Mafiosi tomcat bosses of the area—a mangy yellow specimen called Don Peelee-Billee turned up and gazed balefully at them, his tail lashing.

'Well, well, well—what do we have here now?' he meowed, his yellow eyes slitting evilly. Then he leapt fluidly up several times making their cage swing madly as he batted it with his paws and tried to prise open the door. Poor Gouri and Chiddy nearly had a heart attack.

'Come on out, sweeties!' he yowled hideously. 'Come to big daddy! You'll be delicious, garnished with a sprig of parsley! Don't be shy!'

Gouri and Chiddy clung on to the swinging cage for dear life. Luckily Happy had come running and seen off Peelee-Billee with a snarly 'growwfff'!

'Call me whenever he shows his face!' he warned. 'He and Chhota Chiddiyakhanewala are the scourges of this area. They've accounted for more than 300 birds this year itself. They're serial bird-killers!'

'Who's Chiddiyakhanewala?' Chiddy asked.

'Peelee-Billee's rival and arch enemy. They used to be chuddy-buddies but they fell out over a kitty. Now they're battling it out for power and territory and all the kitty cats in the area.'

And sure enough, one evening, when Happy had gone for his walk, Chhota Chiddiyakhanewala paid the little red sparrows a visit too. It was not a pleasant visit.

'Hello, my little ones, what are you doing inside that horrible cage? Won't you come out to play and join me for high tea, ha-ha-ha?' He was a ghastly slime-green tom, striped in gutter-brown from head to tail-tip rather like a hyena, and had cold green eyes. He licked his lips with a bright bubblegum pink tongue.

Some of the other birds, mynas, babblers and

parakeets who had seen Chiddiyakhanewala leap effortlessly into the verandah now flew around heckling him.

'Nyah-nyah! You're too late, Chiddiyakhanewala! Peelee-Billee has already staked his claim to them! They're his! You'd better make yourself scarce!'

The striped tomcat's eyes narrowed, his pupils glittered. 'Oh yes, is that what you think? Well you can tell that mangy yellow alley cat and son-of-a-pup that I'll be the one dining on these dishy little ones—and he can watch!' His eyes glittered, 'In fact, I'm going to eat them right now!' He crouched down and measured his distance. And then fluidly leapt up, landing right on top of the cage, clinging on to it with his claws, making it swing violently from side to side. Inside the cage, poor Gouri and Chiddy nearly fainted and could only squeak and cling to each other as they rolled from side to side. Luckily the hook and chain by which the cage was suspended was strong and didn't give way.

'Grrowwmmf,' Chiddiyakhanewala yowled and clamped himself to the cage. Claws extended, he tried inserting a paw between the bars, attempting to hook the little sparrows with his claws and scoop them out through the bars. 'Now I've got you!'

'Hutt! Hutt! Shoo—get away from them, you horrible cat!' Ashiana had just returned from school and had come running to the verandah to check on her birds. She had something very important to tell them. Something mindblowing had happened that day at school...

During her history class that morning, she had been staring out of the classroom window bored almost to tears as Ms Sulanewalli droned on and on about how colonized people around the world had struggled and fought for freedom from their oppressors in different ways for hundreds of years throughout history. The view from Ashiana's classroom window was nothing special: just the row of windows of the classrooms in the adjoining block, but then anything was better than staring at Ms Sulanewalli droning on and on monotonously. This morning there appeared to be a lot of bird activity going on under the parapet of one of the windows opposite, and this had caught Ashiana's attention. Little brown house swifts kept flitting in and out from the corner of the parapet. Then Ashiana realized that there was a nest that looked like an untidy clay-pot stuck to the parapet, at the entrance of which a couple of small brown birds clung, looking around with big glowing eyes. The parent birds flitted around twittering excitedly. At last one of the baby birds leapt into space its wings fluttering madly.

'Oh!' Ashiana exclaimed, even as the little bird's sibling followed suit. Both little birds had almost immediately disappeared from sight. Convinced they had fallen, Ashiana got up and went to the window and anxiously looked down, even as her classmates watched her in astonishment. To her delight, she found both the little birds perched on the edge of a parapet two floors below as their parents flew excitedly around them. And then the two little birds were off and flying again, with more confidence this time, zipping and swerving and enjoying themselves thoroughly. Then to her utter amazement they zoomed up and actually perched briefly on her head, clutching on to her red hairband with their tiny claws, twittering softly. 'Oh!' she gasped utterly thrilled, looking upwards as much as she could while keeping her head absolutely still. Then with a little trill the two little birds were off again!

'Ashiana, may I enquire what is so fascinating outside that window?' Ms Sulanewalli icily inquired, imperviously blind to the wonderful little event that had just taken place. 'May we all share in what has so captivated you outside the window rather than inside the classroom?'

'Freedom, ma'am!' Ashiana replied absently, still half dazed, her eyes suddenly bright. 'Th...those little birds...'

'Are you trying to be cheeky? While we learn about freedom movements everywhere, you think freedom lies outside the classroom window?' the teacher asked sarcastically. 'Then you are free to leave the class!' she went on angrily. 'And you may meet Mrs Badi Bandookdum during recess and tell her that you want freedom instead of history lessons!'

Mrs Badi Bandookdum alas was the principal and one who didn't take too kindly to backchat or indiscipline. She was also quite a mastodon of a woman, who often wore frightening makeup, the colour of livid bruises.

'Please, but ma'am...'

'No buts! You will see her in the recess!'

'So to what do we owe the pleasure of this visit, my dear?' Mrs Badi Bandookdum inquired of poor Ashiana after she had presented herself to the principal's dark gloomy office during the recess. 'What heinous crime have you committed now? According to Ms Sulanewalli you seemed more interested in what was going on outside the classroom window than in how the British brutally exploited and colonized most of the nations of the world and then pretended to be all godly and saintly.'

Ashiana looked at the floor. 'M...ma'am...I'm sorry, I got distracted...There were these little brown baby birds sticking their heads out of their nest...learning to fly...And then they just jumped out and flew and I thought they had fallen and died but they hadn't and then they came and perched on my head for a second before flying away again... They were so happy and so brave!'

'And so what did you learn from them, my dear?'

'That it must be wonderful to be free, ma'am, like they were! And that's what we wanted too when the British were here! The little birds were free... and happy.' Ashiana gulped and blinked. 'You see, ma'am, I have two Splendid Rubybirds at home—in a cage... Look, here's a picture...' She fished out her mobile and showed her a picture of Chiddy and Gouri. Her principal (who really was a very good-natured lady even if she looked like she ate children) glanced at the picture. Her eyebrows shot up and she pursed her lips.

'Splendid Rubybirds did you say? Hmm...who called them that?'

'The fellow who sold them to Papa—he gave them to me for my birthday!'

'I suppose the fellow would say that, my dear.

Actually they look like little sparrows that have been painted or dipped in dye, my dear.'

'What? Painted sparrows?'

'Yes. These fellows paint birds like sparrows and munias and even little chicks and sell them as colourful, rare exotic birds.'

'Ma'am, I want to free them. They ought to be flying free!'

'Yes, they certainly ought to be! But my dear that won't really solve the problem.'

'What problem?'

'You see dear, the first mistake your papa made—all for a good cause of course—was to buy the birds. Because once he bought them the fellow selling them would want to go out and catch some more, which he could sell again. If your papa—or anyone and everyone else for that matter—didn't buy any of these birds, well there'd be no point in capturing them, so they'd remain free...'

'I think we should free all birds in cages!' Ashaina said fiercely, suddenly finding she was not at all scared of Mrs Bandookdum. 'And then make sure that no one bought any birds in cages ever again! What's the point of being a bird if you can't fly or be free?'

'Some birds like ostriches don't fly, dear. But yes, they can run around pretty fast and can break a lion's jaw with a kick so they're okay. But some birds which have been born captive—like many of those colourful Macaws and African Grey Parrots—can get into trouble if freed because they wouldn't know how to look after themselves. So it's a difficult problem.'

'If my Rubybirds are really sparrows, they should be able to look after themselves if I free them, ma'am. They can join other flocks of sparrows and learn from them how to be free.'

Her principal smiled at her. 'Well dear, I think we may say no more about your alleged inattention in class. I think this time you have learned more by looking out of the window than by listening to Ms Sulanewalli, don't tell her I said that! But try not to do it again dear, it upsets her. You are free to go and best of luck with your little birdies!'

'Are You Even Birds?'

'Hutt, hutt, shoo you horrible cat!' Ashiana now screamed when she saw what Chiddiyakhanewala was up to. She picked up a magazine from a nearby table and flung it at the surprised tomcat. He leapt off the cage and right out of the verandah with a yowl of rage. Ashiana went up to the cage.

'Sorry, babies,' she said softly. 'I hope he didn't scare you too much.' She gulped. 'You know what

I'm going to do? I'm going to let you go! I hope you can look after yourselves. You're birds and you have to be free no matter what anyone says!' She put a cover over the cage. 'It's Saturday tomorrow. I'll take you to the park and free you there! There's always plenty of birdseed that's scattered around— so you won't go hungry. And you'll be free! Think about that! Now, goodnight and sleep tight!'

Happy came into the verandah and cocked his head, listening. 'Sorry, Happy,' Ashiana told him, petting his broad head. 'You'll miss your friends, and may be sad, but at least they'll be happy!'

And so, the next morning after she'd had her breakfast, Ashiana picked up the cage, slung it over her bicycle handlebars and pedalled off to the park nearby.

'You guys must be very excited!' she told her birds, as she pushed her bike through the park gates and then got on again. 'There's a big feeding platform just ahead where I'll set you free! You won't go hungry!'

Indeed there was. People scattered birdseed,

crumbs, namkeen and other leftovers here, and there were always some birds—pigeons mainly, but also parakeets, mynas, doves, crows and even some sparrows here, along with squirrels, monkeys and the occasional very hungry stray dog. Cats tried lurking around the edges of the area hoping to pounce on a bird, but normally were spotted early and harried away by the others. Now Ashiana approached the spot. The dining area was busy. A whole row of grass-green rose-ringed parakeets, who were celebrating the birthday of one of their number, occupied one side of the feeding plinth, stuffing their beaks and all talking at the same time. Bad-mannered blue rock doves or pigeons just gatecrashed and shouldered their way right into the middle of the table, gobbling and flirting outrageously at the same time. Occasionally a hoodlum crow would flap into their midst with a hoarse 'caw' and cause them all to bluster off. Mynas, slick and wet from a recent bath, would saunter up and see if there was anything for them. Squirrels would try their luck too, darting and nipping in and out, but would be pounced on by the parakeets. There were even a few sparrows—a small flock that ate as fast as they could before whirring off into the nearby bushes.

Ashiana wheeled her bicycle over to the edge of the feeding area. She opened the cage door and gently caught Gouri, who squeaked plaintively. Then she caught Chiddy. With both the little red birds held in her closed palms, she extended her arms and opened her fingers, like she had seen VIPs do on television with white doves of peace, expecting them to fly off immediately. Most of the birds at the feeding platform, having seen her approach, had fluttered off into the nearby trees and thickets and from here watched what was happening.

'Go! You're free now!' Ashiana said, trying to keep the catch out of her voice. The two little red birds however, instead of fluttering off joyfully, just crouched down in her palms and didn't budge.

'Oh!' Ashiana said surprised. 'Are you scared? Okay, here goes then!' She knelt down and gently tumbled the two little birds on to the ground. 'You can fly whenever you want to!' she said kindly. 'Goodbye and good luck! I'll miss you!'

There was a huge frog in her throat as she turned around, picked up her bicycle and quickly rode off out of the park.

On the ground, Gouri opened her eyes and looked around.

'Thank God, she put us down and didn't throw us!' she said, sounding relieved.

'And look where she's left us. There's a whole buffet laid out!' Chiddy said enthusiastically, eyeing the fare on the platform. 'It's an eat-all-you-can buffet!'

They had just begun to help themselves when there was a mighty whirring of wings as the birds in the nearby trees fluttered down. There were parakeets, mynas, babblers, bulbuls, collared, and laughing doves, blue rock pigeons and munias and they all started yelling at the same time.

'Hey, hey, you two—what the heck do you think you're doing?' a hoarse voice demanded.

'Helping yourselves like that!'

'Hogging away!'

'Pigging it out!'

'Do you think this is your father's dining table?'

'And who the heck are you?'

'We've never seen anything like you!'

'Strangers!'

'Foreigners!'

'Illegal immigrants!'

'Terrorists!'

'Do you have visas?'

'Or money?'

'Are you even birds?'

'If you're not with us, you're against us!'

'And you're not with us!'

'So you're against us!'

'Go back to where you've come from!'

'We don't want you here!'

'How dare you eat our food?'

'Go away!'

'Hutt! Shoo! Scat!'

'Go. Never come back!'

Gouri and Chiddy looked around in surprise. A couple of hefty blue rock doves that looked like bouncers had started crowding them and the parakeets, standing straight and tall as soldiers, rolled their eyes at them belligerently.

'They...they don't seem to like us...' Gouri squeaked.

'Push off!'

'Shove off!'

'Or should we throw you out?'

'Gouri, I think we better leave!' Chiddy said nervously as a nasty pigeon rudely shoved him in the shoulder. He took Gouri's wing and the two little birds jumped off the platform and hopped rapidly into a nearby hedge, followed by catcalling and heckling.

'Hah! We saw them off, didn't we?'

'I like their cheek. They just came here without a by your leave and started stuffing their faces!'

'Next thing we know, they'll be claiming the platform as their private dining area!'

'Did you see that? They scuttled off! They didn't even fly!'

'Maybe they're bad at flying. Like the babblers...'

'Abbe, are you saying we babblers can't fly?'

'Yeah, you flutter so desperately...'

'Like you have no control...'

And all too soon the birds at the feeding platform had forgotten about Chiddy and Gouri and were vociferously arguing over whether babblers could fly properly or not.

'Now what?' Chiddy asked his friend as they paused for breath under the hedge. 'We're free, but we can't fly and the other birds don't like us! What do we do? Where do we go from here?'

'I want to go home...' Gouri said in a small voice. 'And I want to learn to fly and be a normal sparrow.'

'Me too,' Chiddy admitted heavily. 'Papa was right. I should have learned how to fly. But...but I don't like being forced into doing anything.'

'Do you think we're far from home?' Gouri asked.

'I have no idea where we are.' Chiddy admitted. 'Let's check out...'

Cautiously they hopped out from under the hedge. The feeding platform was now deserted, and all that was left was a few stale, rock hard breadcrumbs.

'Let's climb up a tree,' Gouri said, 'I don't feel safe down on the ground like this!'

They hopped up to a nearby bougainvillea bush and began climbing their way up. It was dense and fearsomely armed with thorns, so it did give them some protection at least.

'Let's ask any bird we meet where we are,' Gouri said as they settled on a branch near the edge of the bush. 'Maybe they can give us directions home.'

'Yeah, like that fellow up there,' Chiddy said looking up at the sky. A collared dove had risen vertically into the sky. Then it glided round and round in large circles, coming down lower and lower, uttering very self-satisfied 'kuooon-kuooon-kuoon' calls.

'That guy must really get a bird's-eye view of the whole area, like a Google camera or something. He can probably see our nests right now!' And to their delight, the dove spiralled lower and lower and landed right on their bougainvillea bush, quite near them. Valiantly the two little red sparrows hopped their way over to the branch the dove was sitting on.

'Excuse us, sir,' Chiddy began. 'You fly wonderfully. You must get such a panoramic view from that height.'

'Eh?' The dove looked around and eyed them.

'Sir, did you happen to see two sparrow nests numbered 1A and 2A at either end of a verandah on the fourth floor of a building called "Sunshine Towers"?' Gouri asked quickly.

The dove was eyeing them now as if they were something infectious that had crawled out of a gutter. 'And what or who the heck do you think you are?' he cooed. 'Where did you spring up from?'

'Sir, we know that we live somewhere here but have lost our way...'

The dove turned away. 'Oh yes, and the bald eagle is my uncle! Besides I don't talk to strange red birds!' he said rudely and with a great clapping of wings took off.

'Well, well—how rude was that!' Chiddy said angrily.

'Did you see how much face powder he had put on?' Gouri said with a little giggle. 'No bird with so much face powder should have the right to be so rude!' She snorted. 'I bet he's trying to be fair and lovely!' She was right, because believe it or not, the dove's name was Chikna Talcum P.

'Come on, we'll ask some other bird…'

But soon enough, they knew they had a problem. They asked a pair of mynas, who laughed in their faces and took off; they asked a group of babblers, who made some very rude noises and fluffed up their feathers ferociously and bounced threateningly towards them and told them to beat it; they asked a parakeet that hysterically shrieked, 'Get out, get out, go away, go away, you're giving me a panic attack!' They even asked some sparrows, who looked at them askance and raised their eyebrows and coldly told each other, 'Must be foreigners! Bah!' and turned their backs on them. It was clear, none of the other birds were willing to help, and most were downright hostile.

'They don't like us,' Gouri said sadly.

'Because they've never seen any bird as colourful as us! They're jealous!'

'I wish we could fly. Then we could leave this place and go far away.'

'But there would be other birds wherever we went. And they'd all behave in the same way.'

'Maybe not! At least it might be better than this place.'

But Chiddy was right. The news had gone around and with it the message to all birds in the neighbourhood: there was a pair of strangers around—bright red ones—who were trying to pass off as sparrows, but God knows what they really were—possibly carriers of bird flu or some other foul disease, which had turned them bright red. They were to be shunned. Or preferably driven out and maybe eaten. If any owl, hawk or crow were interested, no questions would be asked and in fact, a contract killing could be arranged. But none of the hawks, crows or owls expressed an interest in hunting down the two red sparrows—they too were very suspicious.

meeting at the feeder (where a temporary hunting truce had been called to discuss the matter). 'What are you guys trying to pull? If those fellows carry

But if the hawks and crows and owls weren't interested in a supari contract, there were others

his chops.

way to the feeding platform, as soon as he learned of the contract offer. 'Once I know where they are,

And the fearsome Chhota Chiddiyakhanewala

Billi-ko-Chuha-Banao Couple

Soon the news spread like wildfire. There was a contract out for the two little red sparrows. A contract in which both Peelee-Billee and Chiddiyakhanewala had expressed considerable interest. One thing was certain. The two little birds, whose names were on the contract, were toast. They were doomed.

'We do not tolerate strangers in our midst!' was the firm opinion of the birds at the feeding platform. 'If they are not like us, they are against us

and they have to go. Permanently preferably. The cats will do the job!'

And so it went around: anyone who had seen the two red birds would post the sighting to the feeding platform at once. Both Peelee-Billee and Chhota Chhiddiyakhanewala had (reluctantly) agreed on a truce: they would not hunt other birds here until they had accounted for the sparrows.

When Happy, the big black Labrador, heard the news he was deeply distressed. On his very next run in the park two evenings later he went straight to the feeding platform and began sniffing around. All the birds hastily flew away as he approached— he was after all a gun dog, a bird dog... a retriever. He had to be treated with great respect.

And he was a good bird dog. Sniffing hard he finally picked up the faintest, but unmistakable trace of the scent of his two little friends and began following it. The dye that they had been dunked in had left a distinct smell that didn't vanish easily. It led him first to the bougainvillea bush where the two fugitive sparrows had taken shelter and then beyond that.

Two evenings earlier, when all the other birds were yelling their heads off before roosting, Gouri and Chiddy had come out from the bush they had sheltered under and hopped away as far as they could go. Soon it had got too dark to see and they had huddled together, exhausted, in a heap of dried leaves and slept. The next morning, they set forth again. It really was a strange, if sad, sight: two small red sparrows hopping valiantly over the ground, fluttering their wings ineffectually as they hopped on and on, cheeping encouragingly to one another. The further they got from the hostile birds at the feeding platform, the safer they felt. At last, tired and footsore, they had come to an ancient acacia tree which had lain down during a storm and had never got up again, but which was still living. It was at the farthest corner of the park, quite a distance away from the feeding platform, in an otherwise desolate area. In near darkness the two exhausted little sparrows had hopped their way up and along its horizontal trunk and on to some of the higher branches. Here they had huddled together in a shallow hollow and slept. They rested here the whole of the next day, managing to survive on passing ants, grubs and caterpillars—and a few seed pods.

'We can't stay here forever,' Gouri told Chiddy.

'We can't fly! Going anywhere will take ages! What should we do?'

'At least it seems a little safer here,' Gouri said. 'And there is a little bit to eat too.'

That evening they received a wonderful surprise. Snuffling hard and zigzagging madly as he followed their faint scent, Happy eventually came to a halt at the base of the fallen tree. He looked up, cocking his head this way and that.

'Hey, are you guys up there?' he whined softly.

'Happy!' Gouri squeaked incredulously.

'Happy!' Chiddy exclaimed.

'Are we happy to see you!'

'Yeah, me too! But you guys are in big trouble. There's a contract out for you. Those two mangy cats have taken it. You'd better flee!'

'Happy, but we can't fly!'

'We can't go far!'

'Why do the other birds hate us?'

'What have we done to them?'

Happy sighed. 'You're different, that's all. They haven't seen any bird like you before. They're scared or jealous of you, or both! They're afraid that no one will look at them anymore or maybe bring them food at the platform. People will only want to look at and feed you! You make them feel insecure. They have an inferiority complex.'

'Do you think we're beautiful?' Gouri blinked her dark eyes.

'Umm...colourful yes, but it's not you! The real you! The real you are russet and brown and grey and black and beautifully patterned. I think the real you would be more beautiful.'

'Maybe if we had been painted mauve we would have been more beautiful,' Gouri sighed wistfully, 'mauve or mmm...agenta like a fuchsia!'

'Actually it doesn't matter what colour you are. If you're beautiful from within—that's what counts.'

'Tell it to those hooligans,' Chiddy said sourly.

'Yeah, what to do? They're ignorant and dumb and will always remain so.' Happy looked around. 'Look guys, I have to go now; Ashiana will be looking all over for me. But you take care. And get away from here if you can. Best of luck!'

'Happy, maybe you can help us. Would you be able to find our families? Our nests were side by side, Nos 1A and 2A on the fourth-floor verandah of a building called "Sunshine Towers", Gouri said suddenly.

'Yes, and I have three elder sisters called Champa, Chameli and Chamak. They have very loud voices!' Chiddy added.

'And I have two brothers—Luchcha and Lafanga.'

'If you find them, we might be able to go back home and be safe.'

'Hmm...there are so many buildings with four floors in this city. But I'll spread the word to all the pet dogs in the locality. Some doggie is sure to know if there have been two families of sparrows living cheek by jowl. I'll let you know! "Sunshine Towers", you said? Right then—I'll spread the word!'

'Thanks so much. And thanks for finding us and warning us!'

'No problem, kids!'

Alas, what Happy and the two little sparrows hadn't noticed was that high up in the sky like a spy drone, Chikna Talcum P., the collared dove, was once again circling the heavens and now spiralling down. He saw the big black dog sniffing his way through the park as he followed the scent of the 'wanted' sparrows. Then, as he came lower, he spotted the two blood-red sparrows on the chocolate-chip like acacia.

'Gottem!' he crooned and planed down, 'Now to find those two hideous cats!'

The two cats were at that moment in the middle of a yowling, wailing argument, in the park's car park.

'Those birds are mine!' Peelee-Billee mewled loudly, lashing his tail.

'That's what you think, dog face!' Chiddiyakhanewala responded, crouching low. All he wanted to do was to spring on the mangy yellow tom and tear his throat out.

'Try and get close to them and see what happens, hyena-dung!' Peelee-Billee threatened.

'Yes, I'll take your ears off—that's what will happen!'

They slit their eyes and slunk around each other, yowling louder and louder, working themselves up to a wailing crescendo. Their tails lashed frenziedly.

Chikna Talcum P. spotted them and landed on a lamp post in the car park. (He was not getting any closer to those two psycho-maniacs, truce or no truce. They were out of control and dangerous.)

'Hey, you guys, cut it out for a minute and listen. I've found the fugitives!'

'The fugi...fugi—what?' growled Peelee-Billee, wondering if he could spring on this plump dove. He'd be soft and juicy...maybe too fatty but still.

'Are you calling us names?' the other one inquired throatily. It was quite clear—they were both unlettered and unhinged too.

'Those two red birds who are passing themselves off as sparrows and for whom the contract is out!'

'Where?' growled Chiddiyakhanewala.

'Where?' yowled Peelee-Billee.

Chikna Talcum P. blinked sanctimoniously, 'I can tell you if you both swear never to hunt me or any members of my family for ever henceforth!'

'What?'

'Are you nuts?'

'Sorry, then I won't tell you. Maybe I'll find some other more cooperative cats and tell everyone that you were too scared to go after them!'

'Abbe, you'd better tell us!'

'Only if you promise that I and my family have immunity from being eaten by you both.'

The cats glared at each other.

'Okay—promise!' Peelee-Billee said sourly.

'Promise!' Chiddiyakhanewala muttered. 'But if you give us false information...' The horrible growl died in his throat with a sound like blood bubbling up a windpipe. Chikna Talcum P. shuddered.

'They're sitting just outside a hollow on the fallen acacia tree in the far corner of the park. They're on one of the thickest boughs, two storeys up,' he said, blinking his eyes primly.

'Mine!' snapped Peelee-Billee zooming off.

'Youhavehopeinhell!'snarledChiddiyakhanewala streaking behind him.

'This is going to be interesting,' Chikna Talcum P. murmured. He would have loved to watch the proceedings but he was a dove—a bird of peace. He could not be caught actually watching an act of violence—two tomcats making mincemeat of two sparrows; it would be against the Geneva Convention. He'd lose his good name and licence with the United Nations. 'It'll be all over in no time at all!' he murmured, shrugging. 'Those two don't have a hope in hell!' But, additionally he did give the two killers the precise location where they were, with the help of his personal GPS.

The two little red sparrows had in fact nodded off on their branch in the acacia tree. Meeting Happy had buoyed their spirits considerably. Sooner or later their families would learn of their location and come to rescue them; they were sure of that, because that's what families were for. Then, the very first thing they would do would be to learn to fly!

Dusk had begun to descend, the sky turning to indigo and the first of the moths had begun to dance and glimmer around the park lamps. The great roosting chatter of settling birds suddenly hushed. It was quiet. But so were the two lithe shadows that approached the fallen acacia, first streaking towards it and then, belly-crawling towards the tree trunk in a sinister and evil manner. Both could see excellently in the dim light, and their pupils glowed eerily, reflecting green in the light of the park lamps nearby. Fluidly they leapt up the fallen tree from opposite sides. Both had spotted the little huddled shapes of the dozing sparrows on their branch. Peelee-Billee, his ears laid back flat, belly low, writhed his way up from the right side of the big thick branch on which the two sparrows were perched. Chiddiyakhanewala leapt silently up the branches and made his approach from the left side (no way either of them was going to follow the other). Now they crouched down on either sides of the dozing sparrows, their tails lashing, their ears laid back, their eyes blazing green fire, an evil throbbing gargle burbling in their throats.

'Back off! They're mine!' Peelee-Billee hissed.

'You have a hope in hell!' Chiddiyakhanewala snarled.

Neither was able to control his temper and their wailing growls and yowls grew louder rising towards a crescendo.

Chiddy and Gouri opened their eyes. And nearly passed out!

'Oh my God! We're done for!' Gouri whispered.

'They're on both sides of us!'

'And ready to pounce!'

'Look at their eyes!'

The tomcats' yowls reached a glass-shattering crescendo. Any second now they would both fling themselves on the hapless little birds. And then it would be all over.

Gouri eyed Chiddy.

Chiddy looked at Gouri.

Suddenly, at the same moment, both the little sparrows lunged at each other with their wings, violently pushing each other off the branch.

'Get off the branch, Chiddy! Go! Run! Let them kill me!' Gouri cried as she shoved Chiddy. 'Oh, let them kill me!'

'Scuttle away, scuttle away, my sweet! I will die for you a hundred times!' Chiddy shouted as he gave Gouri a mighty push.

Both the birds tumbled off the branch and began falling.

Then, instinctively, they fluttered their wings as hard as they could, clearly remembering every last detail about flight that Flt Lt Tez had taught them.

And suddenly they were flying!

At that same moment the tomcats leapt. Straight into one another, claws extended, raking at each other's eyes and faces.

Chiddy dropped for a bit and then his tummy seemed to be full of a tumult of butterflies as he righted himself and whizzed almost out of control, zooming up. He hardly realized what had happened. All he knew was that he hadn't landed with a thump on the ground as he had expected. He was still airborne, travelling fast and now a rather forbidding-looking bush was looming up right ahead. Instinctively, he gained height and set his course with the help of the park lamps and looked around.

Right by his side, Gouri was fluttering madly, her pretty dark eyes shining, her wings blurring.

'Chiddy, we're flying!' she screamed. 'We're flying! Oh this is wonderful!'

They had the same feeling you get when you first learn how to balance on a bicycle and go sailing off. And they just didn't want to stop! Using the park lights as their beacons, they flew round and round the acacia tree, watching the shadowy shapes of the tomcats in deadly battle down below.

Peelee-Billee and Chiddiyakhanewala had slammed headlong into each other in mid-leap and fallen out of the tree in a tangle of claws and teeth. They had landed on their feet all right, but were now going hammer and tongs at each other in the dust. This was a do or die battle. Both blamed each other for letting the sparrows escape.

'I had them and you jumped, you clumsy moron!'

'They were mine. You sabotaged my kill! Now I'm going to kill you!'

It was a truly terrible battle they fought. All too soon, Chiddiyakhanewala's face looked as if it had got caught in a heavy-duty blender. Peelee-Billee's stomach had been ripped open and he didn't know whether to fight or to stuff his intestines back inside because they kept tripping him up. And finally, both cats leapt at each other yet again and clamped down ferociously on each other's necks. They dragged each other under a nearby bush, where they died as their sharp canines punctured each other's spinal cords with the killing bites they usually used on birds.

There was no coming back for either of them.

Chiddy and Gouri, after flying several laps around the acacia tree, finally landed somewhat clumsily on the top of the tree and watched the end of the battle, horrified but relieved. Under the bush and in the dust, the fearsome tomcats lay still. The little sparrows fluttered back into their little hollow, huddled together and tried to sleep.

Early next morning Happy came bounding up, eager to check on his little friends. He sniffed around, madly distracted by the pungent cat odour and buzzing bluebottles. In no time, he found the bodies of Peelee-Billee and Chiddiyakhanewala. Anxiously he looked up at the tree, and spotted his little friends who were busy with their toilette.

'Oh my God, are you both okay?' he asked, shaking his shaggy head. 'What the hell happened here?' He sat down, his tongue hanging out a mile out of sheer relief. 'I thought they had got you!'

Gouri shook her little red head. 'No! They came for us but in the end they got each other, which is what they deserved. And they taught us how to fly! I pushed Chiddy off the branch and he just flew. And he did the same to me!'

'But...but why did you push each other?'

'Those cats were about to pounce. I couldn't let them kill Chiddy!'

'I couldn't let them eat Gouri!'

The two little birds regarded each other solemnly. Happy nodded.

'So you saved each other...and learned to fly in the bargain!'

'I guess when you need to do something badly enough you just go ahead and do it, without thinking too much this way and that!' Gouri said, cuddling up to Chiddy.

'Right! I guess the incentive has got to be right!'

'Well these two lowlives have taken each other out...good riddance!' Happy looked thoughtful and scratched his ear. 'Hmm...Okay you two, come along with me. It's going to be breakfast time at the feeding platform soon.'

'But they don't like us...they turned us out!'

'Hmm...' the Labrador grinned. 'I think I know how to change their minds!'

With Happy trotting alongside waving his tail jauntily, the two sparrows flew down onto the feeding platform just as a large flock of parakeets and all the rest of the birds descended to feed.

'You guys, listen up!' Happy said, even as the birds tensed to flee. 'You owe Gouri and Chiddy here, and you owe them big time. You owe them a humongous apology and have to thank them from the bottom of your mean little hearts...'

'What the heck are you talking about?'

'There's a contract out for them!'

'We don't want them anywhere near us!'

'They're red! Must've got bird flu!'

'Shut up and listen! Do you really even know why they're red?' Happy snapped. 'Did you ever bother to ask them? What morons you are!'

'Why?'

'We couldn't give a damn!'

'They're blotched red from head to toe from the blood of their victims! Don't you know who they are? They're the internationally famous Billi-ko-Chuha-Banao couple! They came here after dispatching leopards, tigers, lions and wildcats that had been scourges in other parks. They had heard about notorious Chiddiyakhanewala and Peelee-Billee making trouble here. You, in your foolishness, didn't even wait to listen to their story or ask why they were red. You just turned them out and in fact set those psychos on them. A contract you said. So nice! Since when have birds given suparis to other creatures against their own family? Do you know nothing about clan loyalty? You ought to be ashamed of yourselves! And what did these two gallant, and oh-so-modest little birds do? They quietly took out the cats—see how red they are, covered with the blood of their victims! Go and see for yourselves. Peelee-Billee and Chiddiyakhanewala lie dead beneath the bush next to yon fallen acacia. Killed by these two! Now prostrate yourself before brave Gouri and Chiddy, you ungrateful wretches and do homage to them! Offer them the riches of this table! Be grateful that your chicks will never have to fear those mangy tomcats ever again! Bring your babies to them to be blessed!'

There was pin-drop silence at the feeding platform. Then, with a nod to each other a pair of mynas took off towards the fallen acacia. They were back in minutes, looking stunned.

'It's true!' they whispered. 'Peelee-Billee and Chiddiyakhanewala lie dead beneath the bush near yon acacia!' They ducked their heads in respect before the two little sparrows. There was a hushed murmur all around.

A tall, regal-looking Alexandrine parakeet called Sikander bowed deeply, quickly followed by all the others.

'Huzoor and Begum Huzoor, Your Royal Highness and Majesty, Your Lordship and Ladyship, forgive us for we have sinned and erred!' he said in a deep, gravelly voice he had picked up from Amitabh Bachchan. He bowed deeply again. 'And please do partake of the humble fare at our modest table here...'

'A party! A party! Let's throw a party for our heroes!' shouted a tiny-tot tailorbird in a voice ten times her size. A cacophonous chatter broke out as Gouri and Chiddy found themselves being thrust in the midst of a cheering mob of birds, offering them delicacies from the table. High above, Chikna Talcum P. circled again, looking down in astonishment.

'Kuooon-kuooon,' he cooed, and then, 'Bah! This is just so weird!'

Happy, the big black Labrador, lay down with his face between his paws and watched the celebrations, even as Ashiana came running up.

spotted Gouri and Chiddy in the middle of the

'Oh,' she said softly, dropping a kiss on the big

Homesick for Sunshine Towers

'Hey Chiddy, isn't this just too cool?' Gouri murmured, yawning luxuriously one morning soon afterwards. Then she picked fussily at the fare laid before them. Apart from muesli and mixed dry-fruit 'n' wholegrain breakfast cereal and coco-puffs, there were cherries, grapes, kiwi-fruit, chickoo and papaya.

'Yeah—from being treated like outcasts we're now royalty!'

Sikander, the Alexandrine Parakeet, who had appointed himself as ADC (aide-de-camp—a sort of personal assistant cum bodyguard) to the sparrows bowed deferentially.

'I hope the breakfast was adequate and tasty, Your Lordship and Ladyship.'

'Yes, thank you Sikander. But do try and serve us only melba toast made from wholewheat brown bread—you know white bread is not very good for one!'

'Very well, Your Ladyship, as you wish!'

One huge plus, thanks to this wonderful new diet, was that both Chiddy and Gouri had put on weight and muscle and were no longer the little weaklings they had once been. They were young and strong sparrows.

Indeed, ever since the killing of Peelee-Billee and Chiddiyakhanewala the two little red sparrows were being royally wined and dined by all the birds in the area. What was even more gratifying was that all the other stray and feral cats belonging to Peelee-Billee and Chiddiyakhanewala's erstwhile Mafiosi that had slunk around the locality had made themselves scarce too. To be killed in battle by eagles or falcons was one thing, but to be taken out by a pair of pint-sized bloodthirsty sparrows— that was death with eternal and infinite dishonour! Several birds whose chicks had just fledged brought their babies to the feeding platform and requested Chiddy and Gouri to pose for selfies with their young and to bless them.

'See, that's His Lordship Chiddy and Her Ladyship Gouri. They singlehandedly killed the two most dangerous tomcats in this part of the world. That's why they're red like that! Now come along and let's get a selfie of you with them. Your school admission won't be a problem after that! They're very kind...'

After attending to their needs, Sikander would stand by with dignity as all the other birds got on with their daily chores. Chiddy and Gouri had to lift not a feather—every whim of theirs was fulfilled.

When they flew, a squadron of chirruping sparrows and missile-like parakeets would often accompany them like a guard of honour. Now that he had found his wings, so to speak, Chiddy really did push himself to excel in flight. A visiting peregrine falcon, impressed by the sparrows' reputation, had given both of them lessons in high-speed flight and stooping.

'We really have to thank Happy big time,' Chiddy said. 'He put us on a good wicket!' Indeed the big Labrador had visited them several times and the two little sparrows had profusely thanked him on every occasion.

'We're really lording it over now thanks to you, Happy!' Gouri said, perching on the big dog's head. 'We don't have to lift a feather if we don't want to!'

'My pleasure!' Happy grinned, his tongue sticking out a mile. He turned up quite regularly to check on his little friends and really was a good-natured soul. He winked and wagged his tail. 'It was time these silly fools were taught a lesson! Harassing you like that just because you were of a different colour!'

'Bah! That Happy is such an idiot!' a harsh voice cackled one evening some days afterwards as Chiddy and Gouri preened their plumage on a nearby silk cotton tree. 'He has no idea how much trouble he's got you two into, does he? He can't see an inch in front of his silly nose!' the withering voice went on. Chiddy and Gouri looked around surprised. A pair of spotted owlets, all dusky brown with an attractive pattern of white spots like icing sugar on their heads, were sitting just outside their hollow and glaring at them out of huge golden eyes.

'Err...good evening...and you are?' Chiddy inquired politely as Gouri looked on.

'Myself, Brama—and this is my goodwife Athenabai. This hollow has been our ancestral home since ancient times. You might have heard...' The sparrows nodded, Sikander had mentioned something about a much-respected family of spotted owlets living in the silk cotton tree. Apparently they usually only came out at dusk and were not too popular with the other birds.

'Best stay away from them, Your Highnesses...

they can be unpredictable! They are raptors after all even if they are from a very learned and respectable family with a taste for rodents...'

'And Mr Brama, why do you call Happy an idiot?' Gouri now asked, her dark eyes flashing. Actually she thought Brama and Athenabai looked quite cute, what with their dumpy round heads and icing-sugar spots. 'I think he's a very sweet fellow!'

'Because, I know what really happened to Peelee-Billee and Chiddiyakhanewala! I examined their bodies (it was worse than that—he and his goodwife had had a slap up dinner of Mcatburgers that night!). They killed each other, didn't they? Now have you thought about what's likely to happen?'

'What?' Chiddy asked defiantly. 'And anyway, as long as all these morons believe we killed them—and they do—that's all that matters. I don't think they'll believe you if you tell them anything different.'

'I and my goodwife have no intention of spilling the beans—you can rest assured—we are birds of honour and don't stoop to such things!' Brama said with great dignity. 'But, can't you see what's going to happen? Every bird colony that is being threatened by cats is going to ask you two to go in as exterminators! You are the invincible Billi-ko-Chuha-Banao couple after all! Then what will you do?'

'But all the cats in this area have disappeared!'

'Bah! Delhi's a big place. There are thousands of cats living here. Leopards, even.'

'Well, we'll cross that bridge when we come to it!' Chiddy said defiantly, tucking in Gouri's wing, but feeling a wee bit uncomfortable.

Actually, unbeknownst to him, that bridge was closer to them than he would have liked...

Usually, in the evening all the birds of the locality would gather in the surrounding trees and bushes and exchange the gossip of the day at the tops of their voices. As Very Important Birds, Chiddy and Gouri were given Very Important Perches which were located some distance away from the others, so they wouldn't be unduly disturbed by the noise. They were not to mix with the 'chattering masses' (as Sikander put it, rolling his eyes); it would be unseemly. It would be beneath their dignity to exchange vulgar banter and saucy badinage with the aam-junta, Sikander maintained. 'Madame, the language some of them use...not proper for your delicate ears!'

As a result, Chiddy and Gouri often found themselves all by themselves on their exalted Very Important Perches. While below them, some distance away the birds chattered and gossiped and argued and had a jolly good time.

'You know, Chiddy,' Gouri sighed one evening. 'It really is lonely at the top! I would like to be in the midst of all that juicy gossip, wouldn't you? They seem to be enjoying themselves!'

'Let's join them then!' Chiddy decided. But when they flew into the midst of the masses, much to Sikander's horror, the other birds toned down their chatter and became all polite and proper, bowing deferentially to the two red sparrows.

'This is not working,' Gouri said shaking her head sorrowfully, 'now we're spoiling their fun by joining them; no one's enjoying anything now! We'd better go back to our Very Important Perches!' She sighed and looked sadly at their plumage. 'I do wish we could look just like the others, then there'd be no problem!' In fact the horrible red dye had started coming off their feathers in small patches and all the new feathers growing were of a normal colour. But if anything, the new streaky, splotched red appearance made them look even more frightening and blood-curdling. Spikes and clumps of red-streaked feathers gave them a hawkish, bloodthirsty appearance, as though they had only just dismembered some poor victim. They looked like monstrous creatures from the netherworld who had just taken part in unspeakable blood-soaked rituals. She sighed again, 'You know what I really want?'

Chiddy nodded. 'I can guess...' he said softly. 'You want to go home! You're homesick!'

Gouri inclined her little red head. 'Yes. But how did you know?'

'Because that's what I want too. Not to stay there of course, but just to show them—my sisters Champa, Chameli and Chamak and Ma and Pa and that loud-voiced Flt Lt Tez—that I can fly as well as, if not better, than any of them!'

'Me too! I'd like to see my brothers' faces when I whiz past them!' Gouri said.

'They must have left the nest by now and gone their different ways...' Chiddy mused. 'We'll probably never see them again.'

'Well, now that we can fly, we can search for "Sunshine Towers", Gouri said, brightening up. So that's what they did. Every morning, after a good breakfast, they'd set out on a systematic search-flight pattern, flying up and down in a grid formation, going farther and farther every day. Happy had been right: there were many buildings with four storeys (and more) in the city, which they flew around, but none were the one they were looking for. Happy too had drawn a blank with his doggie friends. They in fact had told him that sparrow nests were few and far between in the locality. Then one morning, Chiddy and Gouri were resting on the top of a neem tree, some distance away from the feeding platform feeling rather disappointed and dejected and wondering if they ought to give up the search altogether. Suddenly a cool breeze gently tugged their feathers.

'Hey, hello kids, haven't we met before?' a soft voice whispered.

'Hello? Who's that?' Gouri and Chiddy looked around but there was no one around.

'Yes, yes...of course I've met you. Don't you remember? I gave you a lift early that morning several weeks ago when you were in trouble and running away from home—and dropped you both down into Murgiben's yard... Nearly didn't recognize you with all the red war paint you're wearing now!'

'Wh...who are you and where are you?' Chiddy asked, wildly looking around.

'Breaking Wind at your service, my dears! You can't see me, but you can feel me.'

'You're the puff of wind that blew us away that day?' Gouri asked incredulously.

'Yes dear, at your service! I had to otherwise you would have fallen and hurt yourselves! I do admit I got a bit distracted and suddenly dropped you without warning—I do get these bouts of sudden, extreme boredom or distraction from time to time, but it looks like it all worked out after all. You're still together!'

Gouri's dark eyes gleamed. 'Breaking Wind, sir... could you do us another favour, please?'

'Anything you like, my dear.'

'Could you blow us back to "Sunshine Towers", please?'

'You want to go back home?'

'Umm...yes, sort of!'

'Okay, kids, here goes! It's quite a distance away so hold on!'

And what had been happening at Nos 1A and 2A, 'Sunshine Towers' all this time? Both Gouri and Chiddy's siblings had indeed left home and were making independent lives for themselves. Their parents were busy raising their second brood of the season. Happily for both the Chiddyas and the Bhurias, their fledglings had settled down in the same locality (called 'Sunrise Estate') and they often met at the feeding station in the playground. In fact they were all now one big (but not completely) happy family...

In spite of Shrimati Chiddya's misgivings about the girls next door being 'fast and loose', Champa had been successfully wooed by Lafanga, and Luchcha had indeed fallen for Chameli!

'I suppose it's all right,' Shrimati Chiddya had told her husband, 'they're both bossy girls and will make the boys toe the line!' Both pairs were now busy constructing their own residences in the adjoining building, 'Suncrest Towers'. Flt Lt Tez Pankha had turned up one morning, glittering with all his medals and ribbons and very correctly, thrust out his chest, and asked Shri Chiddya's permission for 'the hand of your beauteous daughter, Chamak'. His request had been granted. He had been training her for 'Super-cyclone-flying' and while she had excelled in riding the winds like no pupil of his had done before—the pair had been forced to take shelter in a ramshackle shed overnight during a Force V storm which had set tongues wagging... He and Chamak had decided to settle down in the eaves of the villa next door, called 'Sunburst Villa'. Every now and then, Shrimati Chiddya and Shrimati Bhuria would suddenly pause at their chores and think about the two little chicks from their previous brood—Chiddy and Gouri—who they had lost. Then they would hastily wipe a tear apiece and get on with feeding and cleaning their current brood.

They were not the only ones who occasionally thought about the little missing sparrows. Chiddy's bullying sisters too would occasionally remember with a little pang their runaway brother, and Luchcha and Lafanga too would think about the baby sister they had treated so badly. 'We really ought not to have done that!' they regretfully agreed. 'We traumatized the little thing for life.'

It was alas, at 'Sunburst Villa' where the new threat suddenly reared its ugly head, terrorizing the sparrows and other bird families in the whole of Sunrise Estate. New tenants from Singapore had settled in and brought with them a pair of cold-blooded and ruthless kung-fu, ninja killers: a couple of mushroom and dark brown Siamese cats with ice blue eyes, which went by the names Ping-li and Pong-la. There was panic in the estate when the two cats were first spotted, staring frostily out of the villa's French windows.

'We'd better move right away!' Chamak told Flt Lt Tez Pankha as she stared fearfully at the two cats. 'We can't bring up our family in such surroundings! The babies will be traumatized if not eaten!' Sadly she stared at their nearly finished brand-new villa-nest.

But Flt Lt Tez would have nothing of it. 'No one kicks me out of my house!' he declared, jangling his medals and puffing his breast out and strutting around like Generalissimo Mussolini. 'No one! I'm going to check those cats out at the first opportunity, to see if I can find a weakness we can take advantage of. Everyone has a weakness!'

But the panic only spread when the two sleek assassins were let out into the garden. Without delay they set about on a hunting spree that was unprecedented and terrifying. They chose their quarry carefully, selecting only the most healthy, handsome or pretty birds, squirrels and bandicoots (if you can accept that bandicoots too could be pretty or handsome) and took them down with ruthless efficiency: one cat would stalk the target, the other lie in wait to ambush it. What was worse was that they hunted for pleasure, not because they had to; they were fed with imported cat food, mackerel, shrimp, crab and milk three times a day. They were cold and immaculate professional killers—killing cleanly and neatly, with absolutely no mess of blood and gore spread around. They were in fact more fastidious than surgeons. The sight of blood and gore made them shudder and suffer from post-traumatic stress disorders for days afterward—what some soldiers suffer from after returning from exceptionally bloody battles or having experienced humongous horrors over long periods of time on the battlefield. The neat, fastidious cats took their kills to their owner—a toad-like lady with orange hair, shocking pink lipstick and crepe-paper skin who gushed and cooed all over them—and took the corpses into what she called her 'studio'. Her husband was a sleek and slimy looking man with the shifty, hooded eyes of a garden lizard.

One morning a window in the villa was left open and Flt Lt Tez zipped in to 'check out the enemy.' What he saw in the room made even his thick skin crawl, and his feathers to stand up trembling. Mounted on polished wooden plates all along the walls were the stuffed heads of the cats' victims: parakeets, sparrows, blue rock doves, laughing doves, mynas, a glossy magpie robin and even the entire stuffed body of a rufous tree pie, and horror of horrors, an entire family of seven jungle babblers as frowzled up and scowling as they looked in real life!

'Holy earthworm! Are these guys perverted trophy hunters or what!' Flt Lt Tez muttered to himself. At one end of the room was a wooden table with the fresh corpses of the cats' latest victims—a lovely plum-headed parakeet and a fluffed up Indian robin, awaiting their fate. Perched on a fan blade, Flt Lt Tez took in this horrifying scene, just as the door opened and the toad-lady entered, the two cats stalking in behind her. She went straight to the table, sat down, opened a drawer and took out the implements of her grisly trade; cold, sharp stainless steel blades flashed as she twirled the scalpels and picks in her spade-like hands.

'Such a beautiful parakeet,' she murmured lovingly, caressing its soft feathers, 'its head looks just like a plum! Ping-Li and Pong-La you've surpassed yourselves! You choose only the best-looking specimens and you kill so cleanly!' The two diabolical cats purred and rubbed themselves against her legs. Flt Lt Tez decided that he had seen enough and beat a quick, tactical retreat. Now he knew that he and his wife were in real danger, for there was surely no gentleman sparrow as handsome as himself and lady sparrow as pretty as Chamak. These assassins would pin their icy blue eyes on them in no time!

To deal with the problem and inform the others of his discovery, he called an emergency meeting at the feeding platform one evening—after it was ascertained that both the cats were sleeping in the verandah and the coast was clear. All the sparrow families living in the estate as well as some very nervous blue rock doves and several hysterical babblers, parakeets, mynas and bulbuls were present.

'We have to do something about those cats!' Flt Lt Tez Pankha declared. 'They're selecting the healthiest and most handsome birds as their targets, which means none of us are really safe and I and my good wife are probably on the top of their hit list.' He nodded slowly. 'I can account for one of them personally in one-to-one combat, but I will need backup to take down both...'

'There's a recipe on YouTube that says we'll be delicious roasted with deep-fried basil leaves and Thai fish sauce and soya sauce!' Chameli wailed, gulping. 'It's going viral!'

'We'd better flee!' Chamak said tearfully. 'Before every bird in the estate is taken!'

Both Shri Chiddya and Shri Bhuria looked worried: it was a bad business. There was no way they could leave their homes; their second broods had already hatched.

Luchcha raised a wing. 'You know, there have been these crazy posts going viral in the social media about the fearsome Billi-ko-Chuha-Banao couple who have taken down lions and tigers and wildcats everywhere, as well as feral cats. Apparently they recently got rid of a notorious feline Mafiosi across town. Maybe we should try and contact them...'

Lafanga nodded excitedly. 'Yes, I've heard about them too. They're sparrows, but apparently they're covered with blood! The blood of their victims, which never comes off! It makes them invincible. It's said that after killing their victims they dance and bathe in their victims' blood—like we would in a bird bath!'

'Hmm...' Flt Lt Tez Pankha looked skeptical. 'You shouldn't believe everything you find on social media. I hardly think it possible that two sparrows can take down the Feline Mafiosi.'

'Baby, you just said you'd fight these ninja, kung-fu psychos yourself,' Chamak reminded him, clutching his wing, 'but you know you really can't!'

'I can and I will if I have to!'

'Don't be silly, dear. It's not the same thing as flying through flashing fan blades! I think we should let these pros do it!'

'Very well...' Flt Lt Tez harrumphed, 'Luchcha and Lafanga send the word out and try and contact these so-called killer-sparrows. Set up a meeting if you can. Let's see what they're about!'

Unknown to him, the 'killer' sparrow pair, the fearsome Billi-ko-Chuha-Banao couple was already airborne and on their way over to the Sunrise Estate—gusted along by their breezy friend Breaking Wind! But alas, halfway across, Breaking Wind was suddenly caressed by a cute, curly eddy of breeze and went chasing after her—in the opposite direction!

'She's the hottest, cutest little puff that I've ever encountered!' he huffed, hurrying after her. 'We can have baby typhoons and tiny-tot tornadoes together! Such fun!'

'Put us down, you idiot cyclone!' Gouri screamed, all topsy-turvy in mid-air as Breaking Wind picked up speed.

'Can't you focus on one thing for more than ten seconds at a time, you nitwit?' Chiddy yelled.

'Gotta go, kids,' Breaking Wind yelled, 'you just head due north-east, I mean north-west, or is that north-south, or west-east and you'll reach Sunrise in no time! See ya! Wish me luck!' And with that he just stopped dead for a second, gently dropping the sparrows, before he whooshed off at top speed in a cloud of dust and debris.

'Thank God, we can fly!' Gouri exclaimed as the two sparrows recovered quickly from their unexpected free fall and flew under their own power. They settled on the top of a mobile telephone tower.

'Where the heck are we?' Chiddy asked, looking around. 'We're lost again!'

'He said we should fly due north-east-north-west-north-south-west-east...' Gouri frowned. 'In which direction would that be? It's making me dizzy just figuring it out!'

'I have no idea! What a moron!'

'You just can't trust a breeze! They're so fickle!'

'I think we should just stay here tonight,' Chiddy said. 'It's getting dark.'

Some time later that evening, Gouri suddenly felt the soft feathers on her breast being gently ruffled.

'Hey Chiddy...did you feel that?'

'Yeah, something gently stroked my feathers.'

Both the little sparrows looked at each other. 'Breaking Wind? Is that you again?' they asked together.

A cool soothing little breeze caressed their brows. 'Umm...yes, it is! I'm...so sorry for ditching you both again like that...' Breaking Wind went on in a low apologetic voice.

'What happened? You went chasing after that little powder puff—did you catch up with her?' Gouri asked curiously.

'Don't ask!' Breaking Wind gave a little shudder. 'She...she had such a case of halitosis—bad breath, I nearly passed out! She'd just puffed out of a chimney, can you imagine! Belching out of some

little breeze to be with someday,' Gouri said sympathetically.

to take us back to Sunshine Towers,' Chiddy said. 'We have no idea where we are.'

sighed. 'Really,' he went on sadly, 'they should have

Breaking Wind Makes Good

'Whee! This is such fun!' Gouri cried next morning as Breaking Wind lifted the little sparrows high, high, high and whisked them over the city, right above the dirty brown cloud of pollution that squatted over the buildings and monuments, into the clean blue sky above.

'How long before we reach?' Chiddy asked excitedly, his wings stretched out, feeling Breaking Wind under them, lifting him effortlessly.

'Not too long!' Breaking Wind answered. 'Ah, we may be slowing down a little. There's a headwind coming our way; it might get a little turbulent but don't worry!'

It did get a bit blowsy, and the little sparrows found their feathers being tugged this way and that as they were tumbled topsy-turvy like they were in a washing machine. And then suddenly, Breaking Wind blew a giant white popcorn cloud all over them, blotting out everything, but ensuring that they kept together. Eventually it all calmed down and the cloud was blown away and Chiddy and Gouri found themselves being gently swirled around in circles, and beginning to lose height. Breaking Wind was dropping—and dropping them yet again.

'Oh no, not again! Who have you met now?' Chiddy inquired in a hollow voice, 'You're letting us down again!'

'I'm afraid it's more serious than that,' Breaking Wind said, gently depositing the sparrows on a large peepul tree in Lodi Gardens. 'That headwind was bad news—he was looking for you! Apparently a pair of new kung-fu killer cats has arrived at the Sunrise Estate where they're creating havoc. The birds there have spread the word that they would appreciate it if the famous Billi-ko-Chuha-Banao killers took the job of getting rid of the cats as they did Peelee-Billee and Chhota Chiddiyakhanewala. The headwind was looking for you guys! That's why I blew the cloud over you—so that he couldn't see you! You are the Billi-ko-Chuha-Banao couple, aren't you?'

'Umm...I guess...' Gouri admitted in a low voice. 'B...but we didn't actually kill those cats...' She explained in brief what had happened that fateful night.

'I thought so!' Breaking Wind said. 'You see, my cousin sister (who has a diploma in hair-drying) has been blow-drying a lot of Murgiben's chicks and so many other birds that are dipped in dye, so I guessed that's what had happened to you two! But, congratulations! As a result of your encounter with those hideous cats you two learned to fly on your own!'

'But you see, Breaking Wind, we're not cat killers!' Chiddy said heavily. 'And now we'll be expected to kill cats everywhere!'

'And we would so much like to go back to "Sunshine Towers".' Gouri looked obstinately at Chiddy. 'Let's just go and see what happens.'

'We'll be killed by those ninja-kung-fu thugs! That's what'll happen!'

'At least we'll meet our families before dying!'

'Hmmm...' Breaking Wind whistled thoughtfully. 'Do you kids really want to go back? I can blow you to any beautiful holiday destination of your choice!'

'Yes, we'd like to go back home!' both Gouri and Chiddy chorused. They looked at each other. 'Maybe we can fight the ninja-cats!'

'Even if we die fighting them, it'll be worth it!' Gouri said, sounding like a monumental martyr. She gulped. 'I'd just like to see Luchcha and Lafanga's faces when I turn up looking like this! Poor Ma will get such a fright though!'

'And my three sisters as well as that muscle-bound freak, Flt Lt Tez; they'll come running with rakhis, him included!'

'Hmm...' Breaking Wind said thoughtfully. 'Well actually I had a bit of a chat with that headwind. He told me a couple of interesting things. These ninja-killer cats are hugely particular about how they kill—every puncture and bite has to be neat and tidy, with no mess around. They hate it when the Dustwinds—who are my relatives too—blow all over them! Kids, I have an idea... It may or may not work, but at any rate it'll be better than if I just blow you over as you are. Now, you wait here, while I call on some of my relatives and friends... Just hang on here; the gardens are lovely, make yourselves at home!' And in a trice, Breaking Wind just whistled off, leaving Gouri and Chiddy looking at each other.

'Oh my God! Just look at those birds! What are they?'

Gouri and Chiddy looked down from their perches, startled.

A group of people clad in baggy T-shirts and khakis, and armed with heavy binoculars and cameras with huge lenses, stood beneath their tree, staring up at them. The cameras went 'shuttuck, shuttuck, shuttuck' non-stop like machine-gun fire.

'Must be rosefinches!'

'No! Red-munias! Males, six months old who have just eaten gajar-ka-halwa!'

'Rubbish! Must be some warbler species.'

'Warblers? Are you nuts?'

The arguments raged back and forth as Gouri and Chiddy exchanged glances, getting a little perturbed by the attention they were drawing. Also they didn't like those huge cannon-like things being aimed at them making strange noises that sounded like firing.

'I think we should fly away!' Chiddy said nervously.

'No way, Chiddy, don't forget: we're ninja sparrows!

We took out the cat Mafiosi and what we did to the cats, we can do to these idiots!'

She was partially right because actually the 'idiots' were getting extremely annoyed and angry with each other as they argued. It didn't really seem necessary for the little ninja sparrows to swing into action.

'Hey, let's call the TV channels,' someone said.

'Yes, but don't forget it was me who spotted them first!' a scrawny looking fellow declared. 'So if they're a species new to science the credit should go to me! Maybe they'll name the birds after me!'

'You have a hope in hell! They'll probably name it after the Prime Minister.'

'But man, oh man, imagine a new species of bird discovered here in Lodi Gardens.'

'This is going to be so big. Better email the Bombay Natural History Society and the Royal Society for the Protection of Birds and the Wildlife Institute of India and...'

'Just look at them,' a big woman said, 'they're

so small and look so fierce. As if they've just taken down an eagle-owl! All covered with blood and gore.'

'Hey, we'd better check the books first,' someone else said, 'just to make sure.'

So they opened their books and shuffled through the pages.

'No! Not here! And this bird book has illustrations of all the birds found in India so far!'

'So they are something new!'

A fellow with a loud voice and very little hair and big spectacles was looking thoughtful.

'You know, we've taken a lot of photographs,' he said, 'but I don't think that's going to be enough to convince those hard-boiled scientists that these are a new species.'

'What are you saying?' a hatchet-faced woman asked. 'You mean?' She looked at him askance. 'Are you thinking what I'm thinking?'

'Yes, if they're a species new to science then so far they don't come under the species which have been listed as protected. So...'

'So how?' the woman said, eyeing Chiddy and Gouri in a manner which made them both rather uncomfortable.

The man looked around furtively. The querulous group had begun to disperse. They had so far only seen twenty-five species on this trip to the gardens as against twenty-nine on their previous trip and could not possibly go back home having seen fewer. Their bird list just had to be longer.

'Let those morons move away,' the man said softly, 'they have the attention span of fleas. Then we'll take these two down.' He reached in his pocket and took out a 0.22 pistol and a catapult.

The lady eyed him warily. 'Are you always armed when you go birdwatching?' she asked.

'Of course! There are all kinds of weird and nasty types you might meet while peering into bushes for birds. Now we take these two pretty ones down and send their bodies to the BNHS where they can be DNA analyzed and then named after us!' He handed her the catapult and a couple of ball bearings.

'Why should you get the pistol and I get the catapult?' she asked, her eyes flashing.

'Because I have an arms licence,' he responded smugly.

Gouri and Chiddy really didn't realize they were in danger. The huge cannon-like camera lenses had been pointed at them and nothing bad had happened. So they peered down curiously as the man and woman lounged around aimlessly under their tree waiting for the coast to be clear so they could shoot them.

'These stupid gardens are always so crowded!' the man grumbled. 'It looks like the whole of Delhi is here, loitering around with nothing to do!'

'Patience!' the woman said unctuously, 'all hunters must have patience!' She smirked.

'It's a wonder those birds haven't flown away so far,' the man said peering up to make sure Gouri and Chiddy were still there. He paced up and down. 'Damn dog-walkers!' he muttered as a little girl with a big black Labrador started playing with a Frisbee in the lawns nearby. For, yes, Ashiana had brought Happy the big black Labrador to the Lodi Gardens with her mom for a treat. Suddenly, Gouri and Chiddy spotted them both.

'Look! It's Happy!' Gouri cried, fluttering her wings in delight.

'Let's go and say hello!' Chiddy said excitedly.

'Oh my God, they're getting ready to fly!' the man said as the lady looked up in alarm. Both of them threw caution to the winds and raised their weapons.

'Wait!' Gouri said, nudging Chiddy's wing. 'Let Happy run around a bit—then when he gets tired and flops down with his tongue hanging out we'll fly down on his head and surprise him!'

'Sure!'

It was a bad decision.

Ashiana threw the Frisbee and it curled and curved—whisked off by a current of breeze—straight towards the nasty couple. It hit the woman on her arm, upsetting her aim. Happy came charging up and then braked to a standstill as he saw the man with the pistol getting ready to fire. He was a gun dog. He looked up at what the pistol was aimed at and knew what was about to happen. And then he gave a mighty bark and cannoned straight into the fellow. The pistol fired harmlessly, the man yelled and a security guard nearby suddenly saw what was happening and came running up.

'Happy!' Ashiana screamed, appalled that her sweet dog had apparently attacked someone in the park. Then she saw the pistol and the security guard run up and catch the man. Happy sat down at the bottom of the tree, wagging his tail and suddenly, there were both Gouri and Chiddy perched on his big broad head, chirruping away. Ashiana stared in delight.

'Happy! You found them again! Your little birdie friends! I can't believe it! I'm so happy I set them free!' She opened her backpack and scattered some namkeen around.

'There you go, babies! I knew you'd be fine!' she said, quickly taking a picture with her mobile.

'Kids,' the big dog said, gently shaking his big

head, 'you guys gotta be careful. Never trust strangers! Those two were going to shoot you!'

'Oh!' Chiddy said chagrined. 'Why does everyone have it in for us?'

'I'm so homesick,' Gouri sighed, suddenly realizing what a close call they had had. 'I really want to go home!'

Gouri and Chiddy were not in fact the only ones feeling homesick. The killer Siamese cats, Ping-li and Pong-la, were sorely missing the tropical mugginess and sterile cleanliness of Singapore where they had been born and bred.

'Ugh!' Ping-li said, fastidiously shaking a paw. 'Everything's so grungy and filthy here!' Both the cats spent an inordinately long time doing their toilette—especially after they had made a kill. Then they licked themselves thoroughly from ear-top to tail-tip at least six times over, shuddering delicately all the time.

'I wish we were back home! This place sucks! It's a wonder we haven't yet caught some foul, killer infection!'

'The hunting's not too bad, but you can't remain in a jungly place all your life! It's like living in 2000 BC!'

'Some of the birds here are quite pretty, but many of them really need to bathe more often.'

'In Singapore they would have forcibly been shampooed, and hosed down twice a day at least!'

'Or taken to Changi prison and been disinfected, if not quarantined!'

'Remember that fantastic trip we took to Jurong Bird Park?' Ping-li sighed.

'Yes, we really got some neat killing done that day in the aviaries!'

'And now we're stuck here. This house must be at least fifty years old and is falling apart! How Ma'am can bear to live here just beats me! It's like living in a cave!'

'At night it's so scary here! So many creaks and whispers and strange scuffling sounds...I wouldn't be surprised if it's haunted.'

'Do you think the ghosts of all the birds we've killed here will get after us?'

'Maybe...this is an ancient land after all...steeped in legend and hearsay, and full of monsters and demons!'

Their formidable mistress and her husband walked into the room.

'Ah, there you are, kitties! Come to mama!' The lady sat down and plumped both the cats into her lap. 'Now listen babies, we have to brief you: In future you should only try to hunt down sparrows! They're getting very rare all over the world and soon might just well go extinct—like what happened to the vultures. Then the prices offered for their skins by museums and collectors will go through the roof! They'll auction them in all the famous auction houses around the world along with glittering diamonds! If you kill enough and we stuff them, we'll be rich!' Her husband held up pictures of sparrows for them to see.

'You've killed a few of these—but we want you to kill as many as you can! The sooner they go extinct the better! You'll have a treat of smoked salmon and golden fried jumbo prawns every time you kill one of them and bring it to us!'

Ping-li and Pong-la eyed the pictures and glanced away. They had immediately recognized the birds. When they were alone again they discussed the matter.

'Ma'am's right you know! There are not too many sparrows left,' Ping-li said.

'Well, to start with, there's that pair that has a nest up in the eaves, but it's out of reach for us,' Pong-la said. 'They should be our first priority—the cheek of them; living right under our noses like that!'

'Hmm...if we can't get at the nest maybe we can get them when they're feeding.'

'We'll keep a watch on the feeding platform.'

That evening, as they were prowling around in the garden, just after sunset, they suddenly froze. A damp icy breeze made the hair on their ears shiver and stand up, and then it seemed to whistle deep into the innermost channels of their ears, making them tremble and shudder. 'Beware!' a cold, clammy voice whispered virtually inside their brains, 'You have spilled innocent blood! Now the hideous, blood-covered Billi-ko-Chuha-Banao killers seek revenge and are coming for you! Beware! They... are...coming! They are coming to bathe in your blood and to dance with your skulls!'

Both cats shivered and shot up and swivelled around in mid-air, trying to shake off the invisible apparition that had whispered these terrible words. There was nothing to be seen.

'Who...who are you? Sh...show yourself!' Ping-li said, his fur standing up on end as though electrified.

'You cannot see me!' The voice gurgled. 'My name is Ill Wind! I blow nobody any good! You have been warned. Begone by sunrise!'

There were strange unfamiliar winds blowing in Lodi Gardens too. Gouri and Chiddy had dozed off on their peepul tree, when the leaves of the tree began rustling, and awoke them.

'Hey kids, wake up! Meet my friends!' Breaking Wind was back.

'Friends? What friends?'

'Badhair Wind, my cousin! I told you she has a diploma in hair drying! And Jumble-Tumble Wind and Huff 'n' Puff Wind…and Bhootbangla Wind. All dear family members.'

'It's nice to meet them of course, but what are they doing here?'

'Just sit tight on your branches and don't worry about anything! Keep as still as you can! Close your eyes and relax!'

It was one of the strangest experiences of the sparrows' lives. They could feel the breezes tug and pull at their plumage, ruffling and mussing up their feathers, and murmuring to each other as they worked. Sometimes the breeze was dry and husky and at other times, damp and chilly. Sometimes they were pummelled around, at others, softly massaged. At last, as dawn was beginning to break, the breezes suddenly stopped.

'Done!' Breaking Wind said, sounding pleased. 'Guys, you've done a great job!'

'Wasn't such a problem, bro,' a strange breeze whispered hoarsely. 'They were looking pretty gruesome right from the word go—what with all that red stuff on them!'

Gouri and Chiddy looked at each other and recoiled in horror!

'Oh God, you're looking gross!'

'You're pretty revolting too! Scary as hell!'

'What have they done to us? We look diseased!'

'And mad!'

Breaking Wind however seemed very pleased with how they looked. 'Great!' he exclaimed, 'You look great! Like proper rakshas sparrows! Okay kids, now remember one thing: don't touch a feather on your heads. Don't mess anything up. Got it? Okay, I'll fly you home now.' And with that, he lifted the now hideous little red sparrows up again and whisked them away.

'Okay kids, here we are, back in Sunrise Estate. Your building, "Sunshine Towers" is coming up right ahead. Go and meet your families. I'll be off now.' Breaking Wind sounded a little diffident as he dropped the two little sparrows on the top of a tall fish-tail palm near the playground and feeding platform.

'Don't you want to stay and watch the great

family reunion?' Gouri asked, 'The return of the prodigals?'

'Though those guys are probably going to freak when they see how we're looking!'

'Umm...no, I can't hang around,' Breaking Wind said. 'Actually, I left this breezy little thing who I promised to take out for breakfast back in the herb garden in Lodi Gardens, so I'd better be going...'

'Best of luck, Breaking Wind!' the sparrows chorused.

'To you too—I'll be back to check on you as soon as I can!' And with that he was off.

Gouri and Chiddy looked down at the feeding platform.

'The place looks just the same,' Gouri said. 'It's like we never left.'

'And look, they're gathering down there for breakfast as usual!'

Chiddy looked at Gouri. 'Should we join them?' he asked.

'Let's just wait a bit...our families are not there as yet...'

'Sleepyheads! Those fat pigeons will scoff everything up!'

Suddenly Chiddy clutched Gouri's wing. 'There— see those two sparrows that have just come down? That's Chameli and Champa, my sisters...with those two guys...'

'Chiddy, those guys are my brothers! Luchcha and Lafanga!'

'They're big guys, aren't they?'

'And your sisters are very pretty too!'

'Look, there's Chamak! And she's flown down with Flt Lt Tez!' Chiddy rolled his eyes. 'I guess it was bound to happen. She always had a thing for him. I can't believe it! The dude's wearing his medals even for breakfast!'

They watched, unseen, even more thrilled as their parents flew down to the feeding station too. It was getting pretty crowded.

From under a mehendi hedge nearby, the breakfast gathering was being watched by two pairs of ice-blue eyes. Ping-li and Pong-la!

'I don't know about you, Pong-la, but I had the most hideous nightmare last night. Something about bloodthirsty sparrows coming to get us...' Ping-li said softly.

'Me too! It was very windy too. About some cat killers. Must have been something we ate.'

'Well,' said Ping-li, flicking a glance at the breakfasting sparrows. 'The hunting looks good today.'

'Let's go for the best one—Ma'am will be happy!'

'That fellow with the medals and his wife. He's the one who has the pad up in the eaves.'

'Right, I'll go for him, you take the dame.'

'Roger that!'

And then, before he knew what had happened, Flt Lt Tez suddenly found himself sprawled on his back, his wings outspread, staring into the cold blue eyes of one of the ruthless Siamese cats he had vowed to single-handedly take down! And poor Chamak found herself pinioned by a heavy soft paw, which had just begun to prick her soft plumage, ever so softly as the needle-claws were unsheathed. There was a flurry and bluster as all the other birds took off.

From their perch high up on the fish-tail palm, Chiddy and Gouri looked down in horror. They exchanged glances.

'We just have to!'

'Yeah, they've got my sister and that Flt Lt Mr Hero!'

'We are the Billi-ko-Chuha-Banao couple after all!

'That should count for something!'

'I hope!'

'Let's go!'

And then suddenly, Ping-li, who was grinning evilly at Flt Lt Tez felt a sudden hard peck on the top of his head and Pong-la felt something sharply stab her ear as she teased Chamak.

'Eeearrgh!' Chiddy yelled, landing in front of Ping-li.

'We're the Billi-ko-Chuha-Banao killers!' shrilled Gouri, fluttering her wings.

'Oh my God!' Ping-li and Pong-la whispered in terror, staring; their pupils dilated as they stared at the apparitions in front of them. Their nightmares were coming true! The creatures in front of them might have been diminutive, but then so are trolls and hobgoblins and so was Rumpelstiltskin. Breaking Wind and his cousins had done a stupendous job in making the two little red sparrows look as hideous and frightening as possible by blowing their feathers this way and that—their plumage was now standing up on end, spiky as a porcupine and still all bloody and streaked with the red dye. Gouri had a chilling red gelled look that made her look completely psychotic. Chiddy looked as if he had just emerged from the innards of a Gila monster!

'We just finished off a monitor lizard next door!' Chiddy shrilled.

'And are hungry for cat food!' Gouri screamed.

Ping-li and Pong-la didn't wait to hear anything more. Fluidly they turned and fled back into 'Sunburst Villa', streaking under the bed where they lay trembling.

Outside, Flt Lt Tez Pankha gingerly got to his

feet and looked around. He saw Chiddy and his eyes widened. Chiddy had hopped over to Chamak and was helping her to her feet. Chamak at last opened her eyes. She looked at Chiddy and her eyes rolled back up in her head and she fainted.

'Hey Chamak, it's me, your brother!' Chiddy said.

'Y...yy...you're that pp...pipsqueak brother of hers?' Flt Lt Tez inquired incredulously. 'You look like some kind of demon!'

There was a whirring of wings as the others flew down.

'Hi Luchcha, hi Lafanga!' Gouri said chirpily going up to her brothers—who hurriedly backed away. 'Don't worry, babas, I won't eat you! It's me, Gouri—your kid sister! Remember?'

'You...you can't be Gouri! Not...not with that attitude!'

'You'd better believe it, bhaiyya!'

She sidled up to Chiddy and whispered in his ear. 'You know, my knees were knocking when we flew down to attack those cats!'

'Mine were too! My heart's still doing about 2,000 bpm!'

'We had no choice!'

'I guess when you have to do something you just do it!'

Both their parents had flown down too.

'Chi...Chiddy beta, is that really you? Oh, beta what have they done to you?' Chiddy's mom wailed and burst into tears. 'You're covered in blood! Does it hurt, darling?'

'I'm fine, Mom!'

Gouri's mom hopped up close to Gouri and peered at her disbelievingly.

'Gouri, you can't go around looking like that!' she shrieked, appalled. 'Just what will everyone say? You're disgraceful! Go and have a bath—at once!' Then her eye fell on Chiddy. 'And that goes for you too, young man! Going around with my lovely daughter looking like a bloodthirsty roc! Get cleaned up both of you—at once! You're a disgrace!'

Chiddy hopped over to Gouri. 'You know Gouri, maybe we should do as your mom says! Or we're going to be in big trouble! Besides we haven't bathed even once since we were painted!'

So they bathed, and to their great delight, the red-dye (which was really a cheap water-solvent brand) washed off completely. Then Breaking Wind turned up again with his herb-garden breeze (smelling of peppermint) and his hairdryer-diploma-holding cousin in tow. She very kindly blow-dried both the sparrows and restyled their messed up feathers till they looked absolutely spiffing.

'Wow! You really are very pretty!' Chiddy said looking at Gouri as if he were seeing her for the first time.

'And you're some handsome dude!' Gouri said, taking his wing.

They looked at each other. 'You know,' they both said, 'I kind of miss our old scary red sparrow selves! Now we're just like every other sparrow!'

Some days later, the Immigration and Customs officers at Changi Airport in Singapore stared at the passengers who had just disembarked from a

was a pair of sleek Siamese cats, whose passports

passports were duly stamped and they walked on,
tails held high.